Readers love
DIRK GREYSON

Dawn and Dusk

"…packed with suspense, intrigue, action, danger, and the ongoing and edgy connection between Day and Knight."

—The Novel Approach

"This is a must read for any that love romance that's worked for, mystery and suspense, and two men that love hard, sex hard, and carry guns."

—House Millar

Darkness Threatening

"…a worthy follow-up and a fabulous HEA…"

—Prism Book Alliance

Sun and Shadow

"Another winner from Dirk Greyson. I loved the mystery and suspense in this book, but what I love the most was the connection between Day and Knight."

—Inked Rainbow Reads

Challenge the Darkness

"Wonderful story, the flow and pace is perfect and kept me enthralled from beginning to end…"

—TTC Books and More

By DIRK GREYSON

An Assassin's Holiday
Flight or Fight

DAY AND KNIGHT
Day and Knight
Sun and Shadow
Dawn and Dusk

YELLOWSTONE WOLVES
Challenge the Darkness
Darkness Threatening

Published by DREAMSPINNER PRESS
www.dreamspinnerpress.com

FLIGHT OR FIGHT

DIRK GREYSON

Published by

DREAMSPINNER PRESS

5032 Capital Circle SW, Suite 2, PMB# 279, Tallahassee, FL 32305-7886 USA
www.dreamspinnerpress.com

Flight or Fight
© 2016 Dirk Greyson.

Cover Art
© 2016 L.C. Chase.
http://www.lcchase.com
Cover content is for illustrative purposes only and any person depicted on the cover is a model.

ISBN: 978-1-63477-730-8
Digital ISBN: 978-1-63477-731-5
Library of Congress Control Number: 2016906845
Published August 2016
v. 1.0

Printed in the United States of America
∞

This paper meets the requirements of
ANSI/NISO Z39.48-1992 (Permanence of Paper).

For Rhys Ford. You are amazing,
and this story wouldn't exist if not for you.

CHAPTER 1

MACKENZIE "MACK" Redford was tired.

"Gloria, I'm done at the Stevens's place," he said into the car radio as he drove like dust in a cyclone. He slowed when he saw how fast he was going and remembered he needed to set a good example when he wasn't out on a call.

"How bad was it?" Gloria asked.

"You don't want to know." Domestic calls were the worst.

"I think I need to, Sheriff," Gloria said, and Mack remembered that Elise Stevens was Gloria's cousin. Hell, in this area of Central South Dakota, everyone was related to most everyone, knew everyone else, and relied on one another. He liked to think of it as small-town living at its best. But Hartwick had its share of problems, and this morning one of them had reared its ugly head.

"You know I can't on the police band." He needed to keep as professional as possible, even though he'd wanted to rip Harley Stevens's head off. "Have there been any other calls?"

"Not at the moment," Gloria answered. Then the radio went quiet, but his cell phone began to ring, and he knew he'd better answer it or there would be hell to pay. Gloria was a nice enough woman, but mess with her family and she was the biggest mama bear on the planet. "You're not on the police band now, so tell me what that piece of shit my cousin is married to did this time."

"He got drunk and knocked Elise around. She has some bruising, but she kept saying it was from falling down the stairs. If she'd press charges, I'd go after Harley with everything I have, but she won't."

"Hell…," Gloria swore. "I thought she would this time after I had a talk with her."

"She's more scared of losing him and having nothing than she is of him." Mack knew fear, and it had rolled off Elise in waves, even

1

as she'd stood right next to her abuser. "It's a damn shame, because she's a kind person. Gloria…."

"I know. I'll wait a day or two and have a talk with her. I have one more button to push, but it's the nuclear one. Thanks for doing what you can." Gloria ended the call, and Mack continued toward the small center of town.

Hartwick, South Dakota, wasn't much: a single traffic light and a block or so of businesses that serviced the town and surrounding area. The town's lifeblood was whatever the fertile South Dakota soil that surrounded them would produce. Most of the area was cattle country, where hearty crossbreeds were raised. In general it made for a quiet but hard life that led to more than its fair share of alcohol abuse. Firewater, as his grandfather had called it to warn him away and to help connect him to his roots, was almost a plague in his town, and Mack had just witnessed one of the symptoms.

His intention was to make a pass through town and stop at the liquor store to pay them a visit. Not that his professional problems were their fault, exactly, but it was best they knew he was watching whom they sold to.

"Sheriff." Gloria's voice came through the radio like sandpaper, and he was happy as hell to be in his car at that moment. She'd be fuming for hours yet. "A call came in on that anonymous hotline the state put in. They called us. It seems there's some sort of disturbance at the old Richardson place."

Mack pressed the brake and pulled off the road. "I thought that was empty." Shit, that could mean someone was trying to use the house as temporary shelter or for God knows what.

"That place is a mess."

"It looked fine the last time I was by," Mack said as he turned around and headed back out the way he'd come, making a right turn at the first road and then stepping on the gas.

"I don't mean a physical mess. It's an estate mess, or at least it was for a long time."

"Okay. Thanks. I'm on my way." He continued driving as fast as he dared. He didn't want to make a big deal of it yet. He'd received calls through the state hotline before, and they usually turned out to be nothing.

Mack slowed as he approached the ranch. A truck so shiny the sun reflecting off it was nearly blinding stood near the house, and a man was on the porch, huddled over something. Mack pulled up and was instantly on his guard.

The man rose, and Mack pulled his gun, opened the car door, and stood behind it. The man's shirt was covered in blood and a body lay on his porch. From the look of the body and the amount of blood, it wasn't going to move on its own ever again. "Step back and keep your hands where I can see them," Mack called forcefully.

The man was on his knees, and he backed away, putting his hands in the air, pale as a sheet and slightly green around the gills. "I didn't kill her."

"Gloria, I need backup at the Richardson ranch, now," Mack said into the radio.

"Roger, Sheriff," Gloria said. "Deputy Morris is on his way," she told him thirty seconds later.

"ETA?"

"Two," Gloria returned. "He says he's flying." There were few people Mack had ever met who drove as fast as Zeb Morris. He had a love for speed, and it was coming in handy now.

"Settle down and keep your hands where I can see them." Mack took in the surroundings. The guy didn't seem to have a weapon, but that didn't mean much. Slowly Mack came around the door. "Lay facedown on the porch, hands where I can see them at all times."

The man complied, and Mack came closer, his heart pounding as he took each step.

"I didn't hurt her. She was there when I came home," the man said feebly. "I was trying to help her, and then you showed up." He was shaking, which was a good thing. A healthy dose of fear might work in Mack's favor.

Keeping an eye and his gun on the man, who didn't move a muscle, Mack checked the body for a pulse. He didn't find one. Shit, blast, and fuck. He made his way to the man and secured his hands behind his back with his handcuffs. "Stand up," he ordered and helped the man get to his feet. His hand warmed where it touched the man, and he nearly let go at the jolt of interest that shot through him. He had to remind himself that he was not supposed to be attracted to suspects. Mack patted him down, finding a set of keys, a wallet, and nothing else in his pockets. "Okay. What happened?"

"Am I under arrest?" the man asked in a stronger tone.

"That remains to be seen," he said, turning to the woman, who lay on her side facing the house.

The man turned around. "Until I am, you can remove the cuffs, as you have no right." He sounded like some Eastern snob and looked the part too, with jeans that were almost indecently tight and boots that no one out here would ever wear, let alone could afford. Like his car, everything about him looked brand-new and costly, right down to the thousand-dollar white Stetson that lay on the ground near the porch steps.

"Fine, but no fast moves, and your hands stay where I can see them." Mack doubted the man was an immediate threat, so he removed the cuffs and stepped back, keeping a hand on his gun.

Zeb pulled into the drive and screeched to a halt, then raced up the steps and slid to a stop. "Jesus."

"Call the coroner and get him out here. I need you to ascertain who she is, and touch as little as possible. He's going to need to see everything exactly the way it is. Once you've done that, get the camera and take pictures of everything."

A fucking murder in his town. That was just awesome. Just what they needed.

"Yes, Sheriff," Zeb said and raced back to the car.

Mack swore that kid never did anything slower than a run. "Walk," he called, and Zeb complied. Then to the man, Mack said, "Why don't we step aside, and you tell me who you are and what happened." He opened the wallet he'd found and saw a New York driver's license. "A long way from home, aren't you, Mr. Calderone?" Mack lifted his eyebrows.

"My name is Brantley Calderone, and this *is* my home. I officially bought the ranch a week ago and moved in on Monday." Some of his holier-than-thou attitude had slipped away.

Mack pulled out his pad and pen and began making notes. "Is there anyone else here?" he asked, still on guard.

"No. The house is kept locked, and as you can see, there hasn't been any activity here in a while."

"So you're saying you bought this place?" Mack asked, continuing to look around. He now remembered a rumor that the Richardson place had been sold to someone from back East. Regardless, Mack was suspicious and kept his back to the house so he couldn't be snuck up on.

Brantley nodded slowly, like he was sizing Mack up. "Yes. I went to town to get some groceries and to look around. I'm trying to figure out what I want to do with the land. I intended to talk to a few people to find out what would be best, but no one would give me the time of day."

Looking the way he did, Mack wasn't surprised.

"When I came back, I saw someone on my porch. As I got close, I saw blood and tried to help her." Brantley motioned down his shirt. "That's how I got this on me."

"Why didn't you call 911?" Mack snapped.

Brantley's eyes widened. "I was about to, and then you showed up and treated me like a criminal. I was only trying to help her." He slowly rubbed his wrists.

"Sheriff, the coroner is on his way," Zeb said, then went about taking pictures.

"I don't even know who she is. All I know is that I came back from a very dissatisfying and unfriendly visit to town to find someone dead on my porch." Brantley did seem confused and more than a little scared, judging by his dilated pupils. But that could be the result of good acting.

"You have to admit that story is a bit far-fetched," Mack said. He said no more until another car pulled into the drive and parked next to Zeb's patrol car.

"What do we have?" Doc Phillips asked as he strode over. "Oh."

"Exactly. Take your time, Doc. This is a murder investigation." The last thing he wanted was to be on the six o'clock news in Sioux Falls because his office had botched an investigation, like what had happened a few months earlier in the western part of the state. That was not going to happen on his watch. "Zeb, stay with him," he said when his deputy came over.

"Sure, Sheriff. I got plenty of pictures."

"Okay." Mack used the keys he'd found to unlock the door. He pulled his gun and did a sweep of the house, which was empty, just like Brantley said. It was also spotlessly clean and filled with paintings, a few Western-themed sculptures, and furniture that probably cost more than Mack made in a year. He made some notes in his book and returned to the porch, where he joined Doc Phillips. "How did she die, Ray?" Mack asked.

"A single shot to the chest. Didn't stand a chance," Doc Phillips answered and slowly turned her over so Mack could see her.

"Renae Montgomery," Mack said, and the doctor nodded.

"My real estate agent?" Brantley said.

"I thought you said you didn't know her?" Mack asked, standing up and approaching Brantley, sure he'd caught him in a lie.

"I don't, not by sight. I contacted her, and she was acting on my behalf to buy this ranch. We talked by phone, but I never actually met her. We were supposed to meet this evening so I could thank her for everything she'd done to help me."

This was getting harder and harder to believe by the second. Mack returned to his car and made a call. "Gloria, call the city clerk's office. I need to know if the Richardson place sold, when, who the buyer was—anything you can find. And if they're closed, call whoever you have to. I need to know ASAP."

"Yes, sir," Gloria said and hung up.

Mack logged into his computer in the car, splitting his attention between the screen and the suspect. He keyed in Brantley's driver's license number and requested a background check. He needed to know whom he was dealing with. The computer came back with very little information. There were no outstanding warrants or tickets. That wasn't surprising, given the fact that, according to his story, Brantley hadn't been in the state very long. Something wasn't adding up about all this at all. He wasn't ready to believe Brantley's story; something about the whole scene didn't seem right. Mack got back out of his car and returned to where Doc Phillips was still going over the body.

"I called for a vehicle to transport her to the morgue, but there are a few things I think you need to see. As far as I can tell, she's been dead about an hour, maybe two. The blood has just started to pool a little. The thing is, I don't think she was shot at close range. I need to get the bullet out and look at it, but the caliber doesn't seem right, and there are no powder marks. My initial guess is that she was shot with a rifle."

Bells went off in Mack's head. "Thanks. Was she moved at all?"

"Only rolled over, as far as I can tell, and from the blood stains, she fell forward and was probably facedown."

Mack nodded and got out of the way so Doc Phillips could do his job. "Shit," he swore under his breath. It would have been so damn simple if this guy—stranger, new in town—had done this. His job would have been easier, but now he was going to have to unravel a puzzle. And the person the town would love to pin it on because he wasn't one of their own didn't seem to have done it. Mack was still suspicious of the Easterner, but as much as he'd like this to be an easy case, Mack would have to check out Brantley's story, as well as run down half a million leads, he was sure. But damn, something wasn't right.

"Let me get this straight," he said to Brantley as he approached again. "You bought this ranch without ever meeting your real estate agent? Did you look at the place?" Mack asked as the morgue truck arrived.

"I saw pictures. Renae came out here and took detailed photos of each room and the view from each window. She must have sent me two hundred pictures. Then she walked the perimeter of the property and took pictures there as well. So even though I hadn't seen the property, I knew the measurements of each room because she also put together a detailed floor plan. Renae went above and beyond for me." Brantley turned and watched as the morgue personnel lifted Renae's body off his porch and put it into a body bag. Then they placed the bag on a stretcher and rolled it to the waiting black coroner's vehicle, which looked a lot like a hearse.

"Why did you buy this particular ranch, Mr. Calderone?"

"I initially saw pictures of it online and contacted Renae once I decided to move out West."

Mack could tell he wasn't giving him the whole story, and if he needed it, he would be back for more.

"I've looked in a few other places, but nothing felt right until I saw this place. There are trees in back and plenty of yard. The barn is in good shape, and I can get horses if I want. There aren't any cattle, but I can change that if I decide to. I thought I might want children one day, and there's a spring and a creek that runs along the ridge. Renae even took pictures of a swimming hole."

"And you never actually met her?"

"No. Not until I found her on my porch. I tried to help her. But there was nothing I could do. I think she was already dead by the time I got home." He tilted his head. "Can I ask you something?"

"All right," Mack said skeptically.

"How did you know to get out here? I'd been home maybe three or four minutes when you showed up, and there hadn't been a car by the ranch at all."

Mack had wondered about that as well. "We got a call through the state hotline. Can you tell me where you'd been for the past few hours before you got home?"

"I was at the grocery store in town. The girl with the green hair and black lipstick checked me out. I'm sure she'll remember me. Oh yeah." Brantley took off toward his truck, and Mack tensed when he opened the door. "I have the receipt here with me, and it has a time on it." He returned and shoved the paper into his hand. "You'll see the corresponding credit card in my wallet, and you know how long it takes to get out here from town. I'm sure the coroner has told you an approximate time of death, so you should have a pretty good idea that I didn't kill Renae. But obviously someone did."

Mack checked the receipt and the credit card, then handed the wallet and keys back to Brantley. "Do you have any enemies, Mr. Calderone?"

"Me? Here? I moved here a week ago. I haven't had the time to make any enemies. All I've done is tried to get unpacked and get the house set up. I've been into town twice, and so far as I know, I haven't looked cross-eyed at anyone. Few people have spoken to me, so I have to say no."

"What about back in New York?" Mack asked.

Brantley's confidence cracked a little. "I was in a very cutthroat business for a number of years. Fortunes could be made one day and lost the next. Thankfully I made many more fortunes than I lost, and those that didn't come out so well? Let's just say they aren't going to be sending me flowers."

"So you do have enemies," Mack pressed.

"Yes. Almost three thousand miles away, and they would be happy that I'm way out here and no longer involved in the business. I retired from financial management and hedge funds when I decided to relocate out here. So any of these enemies would want to keep me out here and far away from the New York financial markets."

"Call me a country sheriff, but I don't understand. People who hate you will sometimes go to great lengths to hurt you," Mack explained. He had seen it more than once in his career.

"That may be, but killing my real estate agent is hardly the way to do it." Brantley shook his head. "No. The men I count as my enemies would be motivated by making more money than me in my absence. See, I have more than I could ever spend in two lifetimes. But that doesn't matter. Money isn't about what you can buy with it. For them, and me up until a while ago, money is simply a way of keeping score. The more you make, the better you are at playing the game, and the less someone else makes."

"It sounds pointless," Mack said. Everyone he knew worked hard to try to keep house and home together. A life like that was unfathomable.

"It was, to a degree. That's why I got out while I was on top." Brantley smiled slightly as Mack continued making notes.

"If you could give me the names of these enemies, I'd like to try to eliminate them as suspects."

"Very well." Brantley rattled off several names. "You aren't going to get anywhere near them. They work all the time and are surrounded by people at nearly every hour of the day for one reason or another."

Mack was clearly out of his depth.

"I never got coffee or took care of mundane things like laundry," Brantley went on. "I had people who did that, including more than one personal assistant. They knew where I was at all times so they could support me and help me remain productive."

That left Mack with little to go on at the moment. He'd have to start by speaking to Renae's family and friends to try to find a motive for her murder. But something still niggled at him. "Do you know why Renae was here today?" He turned toward a dark green Toyota Corolla that he'd seen around town many times. "Did you call her?"

"No. I'm surprised she was here as well. I wasn't expecting her. She may have stopped by to give me something, but I would have expected her to call." Brantley pulled out his phone. "She didn't."

Mack made a note to request telephone records in order to see what calls she had received. "Thank you." He was running out of questions. He went to Renae's car, pulled on gloves from his pocket, and then opened the door. It was neat, with a box of files on the backseat and a day planner on the passenger-side floor. He carefully lifted it out and checked her appointments for today. There wasn't anything noted for the last few hours. "So this wasn't a planned appointment." Mack turned to stick his head out of the car door. "Zeb."

His deputy rushed over. "Sheriff."

"Have you found her phone?"

"No."

"Check on the porch, and be sure to wear gloves. Once you're done, widen the search if you don't find it and then check out in the field and see if you can find where the shooter stood." If it was a rifle shot, then the shooter stood somewhere, and Mack was determined to find where that was.

"Is it all right if I unload my groceries and take them inside?" Brantley asked. "I'd also like to change my shirt, but I'll bring this one to you if you like."

"Please," Mack said. "Don't disturb anything outside."

"I won't." Brantley stared at the spot on the porch marked by the bloodstain. "This may sound dumb, but will you clean that up, or...."

"We will once we have what we need," Mack said.

Brantley went to his truck and carried plastic bags inside, going around the area where Renae's body had been.

Mack carefully checked under the seat, but found nothing helpful. He popped the trunk and looked there as well. Only some For Sale signs and the materials of her job. The car wasn't much help, but he did bag and tag her day planner for evidence. When he was done, he joined Zeb in the search for the phone, but they came up empty. She certainly would have had one.

"I found where the shooter was," Zeb called as Mack was about to give up. "It's about forty yards out in the field." He led Mack to the spot. "The shooter must have hidden behind that building right over there and then stepped out to take the shot. The trail of crushed grass is pretty clear, although it won't be tomorrow."

Mack followed the trail to the end and carefully searched the tall grasses. He'd hoped to find a casing, but there was nothing. The shooter must have taken it with them. He did have Zeb take pictures of the spot, as well as the view back toward the house.

"Are we done here?" Zeb asked.

The coroner had left with the body, and Mack was left with questions and yet more questions.

His phone rang, and Mack pulled it out of his pocket.

11

"Sheriff, I was able to get that information you asked for from Records. The sale of the Richardson place went through a week ago, and the new owner is a Brantley Calderone. They're sending over copies of the documents, and I'll put them on your desk so you can look at them as soon as you get back."

"Thanks," Mack said, watching the house for a few seconds. "Zeb, we're done here for now." He lifted his hat off his head, waved it a few times to cool off, and then plopped it back.

"All right. I'll get things packed away."

"Very good. Send me copies of all the pictures, and I want your impressions of everything from the body, to Calderone, to the ranch." He had long ago learned that others saw different things than he did, and he wanted to make sure nothing was missed.

"What are you going to do?"

"Run down what I can of Mr. Calderone's story." He needed to verify that he was telling the truth. The easiest thing would be to find that Calderone was lying, and then he could close the case. Brantley had answers for everything. Even so, Mack wasn't ready to accept them. Not yet. The best lies and cover stories were those woven with just enough truth to make them believable.

"I'll see you back at the station," Zeb said.

Mack nodded, then walked back toward the house and knocked on the door. It opened to reveal Brantley standing in the same tight jeans and a tank that highlighted the top of a powerful chest.

"I put the shirt in a plastic bag for you." He handed it to Mack. "I'm sorry about Renae. She was helpful and seemed like a nice person. Did she have a family?"

"Thankfully no. She divorced her husband a few years ago, and they had no children." Mack was going to have to tell the useless bastard about his ex-wife's death, though. Not that Harry Montgomery was likely to care about anything other than the bottom of a whiskey bottle. "Please don't make any plans to leave town. This is an ongoing investigation, and it's likely that we'll have additional questions."

"Am I still a suspect?" Brantley asked, a little surprised.

It was on the tip of his tongue to tell him yes. "You're a person of interest. I'll leave it at that." Mack blinked as his gaze centered on Brantley's trim form and incredible eyes, zeroing in on exactly the kind of interest he'd like to be showing. But Mack pushed that down deep, where it belonged. "I'll be in touch." Mack turned and took the shirt back to his car.

CHAPTER 2

BRANTLEY'S LEGS held out until he closed the door, and then he collapsed into the nearest chair. During all of the activity, he'd been able to keep his mind on what was happening and managed to remain aloof, but now everything hit him like a semitruck at freeway speed. Someone had been shot on his front porch, and it was obvious that whoever had done it was either trying to send him some sort of message or it was a clumsy effort to frame him. Either way, it scared the living shit out of him.

He picked up his phone and made a call back East. "Linda, pick up," he said under his breath as the phone rang.

"This better be good, sweetheart. I finally got Jim to take me out to that new restaurant. It took three months to get a reservation, and we have to leave in ten minutes."

Brantley could practically see her hurrying through the bedroom of her Upper East Side apartment. "I came home today and found a dead body on my porch. Someone shot my real estate agent, and I think they tried to pin it on me." He leaned forward, trying to get oxygen to his head. "I lived in New York for God knows how long, and I've spent a week out here, where it's supposed to be open and where everyone knows everyone else, and there's a dead body on my porch." He was tempted to fucking sell the place and go back home.

"Honey, wait. Are you serious?"

"Yes." He held his head and stroked his forehead.

"So come home. We miss you, and those people are obviously weird out there. What, do they kill each other off and put the bodies on each other's doorsteps? Hello, Welcome Wagon," Linda said, and Brantley knew she was throwing her hands in the air dramatically.

"I don't think that's how it works. But I have to tell you that being out here alone is starting to freak me out. I have every door locked, and I'm sitting in the middle of the room away from windows in case anyone is watching me. Have I told you that it's freakishly quiet out here? There isn't a sound except bugs and birds, and at night it's just the bugs. No cars, nothing."

"Then come home."

"I can't. You know that. Everything there has been sold, and I bought this place here." He'd uprooted his life to find something he thought he was missing. He hadn't expected a murder on his doorstep.

"Then get a dog, maybe two. Big ones that will bark when anyone gets close and keep you company. They'll also make noise, if the quiet is what has you freaked out."

"Mainly it's the dead body."

"They don't really think you did it, do they?" Linda asked.

"I don't know. The sheriff seemed thorough enough, but he cuffed me when he first arrived."

"He *what*?" Linda nearly blew his ear off. "You aren't a criminal." Her righteous indignation was part of the reason he'd called. "Why in the hell did he do that? I'd call the local paper and give them what for. Abuse of police power and all that."

"He didn't keep me handcuffed long, but he thought I might have killed someone. I think he did it for his own safety." Jesus, now he was defending the guy. He needed to get a grip. This whole thing had really unsettled him. He needed to find something to do to push this shit out of his mind. He hadn't killed anyone. Fucking hell, he'd barely spoken to a single person in town. "It's all right. Everything turned out fine, and I'm home and not in handcuffs."

"You had better not be, or he'll have to answer to me."

He laughed and felt better. "What are you going to do? Gucci-whip him?"

"Smartass." Linda had calmed down. "Don't let those people intimidate you or get the better of you. No one in New York ever did, and you can't let them do it out there either. So make sure they know exactly who they're dealing with. Get yourself a lawyer and tell this sheriff guy to back off."

"Well...."

"Brantley... is the guy hot?" she asked in that tone.

"Not that that has anything to do with any of this, but yeah. He's a big guy, maybe part Native American, with these piercing eyes that would have you salivating. He's just the kind of guy you would have tried to pick up before you married Jim. I think they grow things big out here."

"Well, like I said, don't let him get to you, and stand up for yourself." She was clearly getting distracted. "I need to let you go. Jim is ready, and we don't want to be late. I'll definitely call you tomorrow, and you can let me know what else happens." She made kissing sounds and then ended the call.

Brantley slid the phone onto the coffee table and turned on the television. Before coming out here, he'd never watched anything other than the various financial news channels to monitor the markets. He flipped through numerous channels to try to find something that didn't completely suck. He'd watched more television in the last week than he had in years. Not that he was interested, but he needed something to make the house seem less empty.

It didn't work very well. As the light faded outside, darkness seemed to close around the house, coating it in gloom that no amount of lights seemed to be able to dispel. He pulled the curtains closed in every room and tried to concentrate on whatever he was doing.

The last thing he thought he'd need when he moved out here was a security system, but now it seemed like a great idea, and he felt like a fool for not having one installed. He made a note to look into it first thing in the morning. Of course, his first hurdle was probably going to be getting someone out here to install it.

At nearly midnight Brantley was on the sofa, watching television, jumping at every sound from outside and getting damned tired of it. Fucking hell. He'd taken on the wolves in New York and come out on top. He'd done battle with some of the most brilliant financial minds from around the world and beaten them. He was not going to let a few noises scare him. He went through the house, turning off the lights as well as the television before going to bed.

EVENTUALLY HE slept and woke to a dark room. He'd purposely hung heavy curtains in the bedroom, and he blinked a few times when he turned to the clock by the bed. It was nearly eleven. He'd made it through the night. He got up and shuffled into the kitchen, made some coffee, and then peered out the front windows.

"That's a win," he muttered to himself when the porch showed no one lying on it. He went back to the kitchen, absently scratching his butt before pouring a mug of coffee and sipping slowly. God, he needed that. Brantley sipped some more, the caffeine finally pushing the sleep from his brain as he looked out the kitchen window to admire the view.

"What the hell?" he muttered under his breath, leaning over the sink to get a better look out the window. Dark shapes were moving across the back of his property. He continued watching as more and more of them passed along the ridgeline. He went to the living room and snatched his phone off the coffee table. Not that he knew whom to call at first. But then he looked up the sheriff's number and dialed.

"Hartwick County Sheriff's Office," a woman said when she answered the phone.

"Yes. Um, I'm not sure if this is who I should call, but there are some animals moving along the back of my property, and they aren't supposed to be there." He wandered back into the kitchen to watch the creatures.

"Maybe there's a fence down. Why don't you call your neighbor and ask?"

"Well, I don't know who my neighbors are. I just moved in a week ago," Brantley said. "I need someone to take a look and help me. They shouldn't be there." And he was wondering if they'd get together and stampede toward the house.

"If you give me your address, I'll have someone come out." She sounded like Brantley had called to ask them to take out his garbage or something, but he gave her the address anyway. "Oh, the Richardson place." Her tone shifted to something more ominous. "All right, I'll alert the sheriff. Someone will be out shortly."

"Thank you." Brantley hung up and continued watching the groups of dark spots as they moved across the field. They seemed to be congregating to the one side of the property. Brantley suspected they were someone's cattle, but he had no intention of going out there to find out. They seemed to stay where they were, and he'd do the same.

By the time he'd finished his coffee, Brantley realized he was still wearing his boxer briefs and nothing more, so he hurried to the bedroom and pulled on some clothes, finishing as the crunch of tires sounded outside.

"What's the problem?" the sheriff asked when Brantley opened the door.

He stepped out into the building heat and led him around to the back of the house. "Them," he said, pointing. "They aren't supposed to be there."

"Probably Erickson's cattle," the sheriff said and got on the radio. "Gloria, can you call Erickson? He needs to get his cattle off his neighbor's land."

"Sure thing."

"Why are they here?" Brantley asked.

"Probably for the water. It's been very dry, and the cattle can smell water. They'll knock down a weak fence to get to it."

Brantley nodded before asking what he really wanted to know. "Did you find out anything about Renae?"

"I was able to corroborate your story and whereabouts for yesterday."

"So I'm not a suspect," Brantley said, and the sheriff nodded darkly. "What's next, then?"

"We're looking into her life. There had to be a reason someone killed her, so we're trying to figure it out. We're pulling her phone records and things like that."

"Do you think you'll figure out who did it?"

The sheriff turned toward him, eyes burning. "Of course I will. Sometimes these things take time, but I will figure out who's behind this and why."

Brantley wasn't sure if that was meant as a threat or not. "I wasn't impugning your investigative powers. It just seems like there isn't much to go on." And he would feel a hell of a lot better if he knew what the hell was going on and why someone thought it a good idea to shoot her on his front porch.

"I know you didn't shoot her, but my gut is telling me that her death has something to do with you." The sheriff continued drilling his gaze into Brantley, and he refused to shiver or back down even though he could feel his insides withering under the intensity.

"What did I ever do to you or anyone here? I never even met Renae. I haven't lived here long enough to make enemies."

"Maybe and maybe not. But I don't believe in coincidences, and though Renae Montgomery wasn't killed by you, someone went to some trouble to make sure they killed her on your porch. We have confirmed that she got a phone call from a burn phone with a 212—New York—number before she was shot. The call lasted less than five minutes, and we believe it was the one to arrange the meeting. I'm wondering if she could have thought she was speaking to you or someone acting on your behalf. She came out here to meet you and was shot." He sounded very matter-of-fact.

"I had nothing to do with her death," Brantley said again. "She was a nice person and very helpful." He blinked a few times. "Why are you telling me all this?"

"Because I'm hoping you can help me. There's a reason she was killed on your doorstep."

"I have no idea why anyone would do that," Brantley said. "I was up half the night trying to figure it out, and I don't know. Maybe they thought the house was still empty and this was a good place to lure her to." The sheriff's gaze made Brantley want to squirm and get away, but he held his ground. Being nervous and jittery wouldn't help him sound convincing, and Brantley knew this was one of those times when confidence and determination might help him. Lord knows doubt could sink his ass.

"I don't think so."

"How do you know, Sheriff?"

"Most everyone calls me Mack. Someone went to some trouble to get her out here, and they knew the house was occupied because we got that anonymous call. Like I said, there's a reason for all this, so if you think of anything, you let me know."

"I will." Brantley didn't know what else to say and took a step back, turning away from Mack's intensity to watch the cattle out in the field.

Under different circumstances, being stared at that way, with such interest, would be thrilling. Mack was hot. There was no doubt about that. But at a time like this, those kinds of thoughts had no place. Besides, he was in the middle of rural America, and ogling the sheriff was a bad idea on so many levels.

"What's that now?" Brantley asked, hearing crunching on the gravel drive. He turned and walked around the side of the house.

"Andy Erickson, your rear neighbor with the fence problem," Mack said as he came up next to him.

"Are you the one who called the sheriff because some of my cattle got on your precious land?" The middle-aged man's eyes blazed as he strode toward Brantley.

"Andy, that's enough," Mack said. "He wasn't sure who to call, so he phoned us. Just drive the cattle off and repair the fence. There's no need to make a federal case out of it."

"Why the fuck should I? We're in the middle of a drought. I'm trying to dig another well so I can water the cattle, and he's got water to spare that isn't being used."

"Now look here," Brantley said, stepping forward. "I'm all for being neighborly, but you can't just let your cattle on my land without permission. It isn't yours and you have no right to it." Brantley took a step closer to this Erickson guy. "So get them off my land—now."

Andy stepped forward, puffing out his chest. "What are you going to do about it?"

"Nothing. But I will," Mack said. "Andy, you need to get your cattle off his land and repair that fence, and you know it. You don't have any rights to what isn't yours, and you know that too. So stop acting like an ass and take care of your business."

"He shouldn't even have this land."

"If you wanted it, then you should have bought it. The ranch was for sale for a while."

"At a price no one could afford," Andy countered.

"Well, he could, and now it's his land." Mack stepped between them. "You need to move the cattle, so get to it. Unless you want me to go out and investigate that fence that they *broke* through." The threat was clear, and Andy blanched but didn't argue the point.

"Fine. I'll move the cattle as soon as I can."

"You'll do it by two, or he can press charges and I'll have to bring you in. And if I do that, I'll confiscate the cattle as evidence. Then where will you be?" Mack put his hands on his hips. He was intimidating and hot as hell. Not that Brantley was supposed to be noticing. He turned away to keep from snickering. He hadn't meant this to devolve into a pissing contest, but he was happy the sheriff was standing up for him.

"I can't believe you'll stand up for some newcomer instead of an old friend whose cattle are drying up."

"We were never friends, so don't try that angle, and it doesn't matter who it is. The cattle are on his land, and he's asked you to move them. There's no need to get angry. Maybe if you'd come to him and asked to graze your cattle for a few weeks, he might have let you. But that doesn't seem likely now." Mack glared, and Andy eventually turned in a huff, stomped back to his truck, and slammed the door before taking off down the drive.

"I guess I made a real impression on that neighbor," Brantley said softly.

"Erickson is a pain in the ass. He has water on his land. The stream that comes off your spring runs through his property. He let his cattle graze there too long this spring and early summer. Now the grass is played out and needs a chance to grow, but he doesn't have

21

any water anywhere else, so he needs to figure something out, and *accidentally* letting his cattle graze on your land is easier than solving his real problem."

"Has it been that dry?"

"Yes. The creeks are running very low, and so are the rivers they feed. Some ranchers have had to sell early because they don't have the water for their herds. These are tough times around here, and you have one of the few ranches with a permanent water source. Each one of your neighbors wanted to buy this place, but the heirs wanted a lot more money than they could afford. At least that was the rumor around town."

"Thank you for your help," Brantley said. "I appreciate you coming out. And I promise that if I think of anything, I will call right away." Ideas were already churning in his mind, but he wasn't sure where he should go with them yet, so he kept them to himself and decided to let them percolate for a while.

"Andy is a bit of a hothead sometimes, but I doubt he'll make any trouble. And most of his anger is going to be directed at me. Just keep an eye out and make sure he drives his cattle home. If he doesn't, call in, and I'll stop by to speak to him. He doesn't want me to go out and look at that fence because it's likely he knew it was weak or weakened it himself so it would fail and his cattle could flow into your land and fresh grass."

"What was he thinking?"

"That maybe if you didn't make a stink, he'd keep them there for a week or so and then get them back. During that time, they'd be eating fresh grass and drinking your water, and if he were lucky, it would rain and his grass would have a chance to recover."

"So...." Brantley's mind was turning quickly. One of the strengths that made him good at his job and allowed him to make massive profits for himself and his investors was his ability to think many steps ahead very quickly. "Is it possible that one of my neighbors was behind Renae's death? With me out of the way, they could buy the ranch up cheap and add it to theirs because few people are going to want it, and then they'd have the water source."

"I have thought about that, and we're looking into it. It seems like a plausible theory, and we aren't leaving any stone unturned." Mack tipped his hat and walked back toward his car.

Brantley watched him the entire time, unable to take his eyes off the way Mack filled out his uniform pants.

Mack got into his car and drove away, leaving Brantley standing outside, blinking in the bright sun. He was completely helpless, and that was a feeling he wasn't used to. He hated it. So he figured he needed to do something about it. He had already met one neighbor, and that had gone over really well. Maybe it was time to go out, meet the others, and see what was going on. Maybe he'd learn something that could help. If it was true that one of his neighbors did indeed want him out, then maybe he could figure out who it was. Andy Erickson seemed perched at the top of the list, but who knew who else might have it in for him because of the land he'd bought. There was only one way to find out.

Brantley turned and jogged into the house. He grabbed his hat and changed into his boots. He wanted to look like he belonged. Then he grabbed his sunglasses, locked the doors, and climbed into his truck. He had some visiting to do, and there was no time like the present.

At the end of the drive, he decided to go right first and test his luck. He drove five minutes or so down the road and turned into the first drive he saw. He passed barns and outbuildings and pulled up to a sprawling ranch house, making sure he didn't run over the small bicycles and various plastic toys that littered the area. He stopped and hoped he wasn't on top of anything. The toys seemed to be everywhere. Brantley opened his door and got out of the truck, then closed the door and looked to see if anyone was around.

"Hello," a young voice said, and Brantley whipped around. A boy about four years old stood on the porch in jeans, a flannel shirt, a small cowboy hat, and boots.

"Is your mom or dad around?" Brantley asked, and the boy pointed toward the barn. "Are all these toys yours?"

The boy nodded. "I maked a mess," he said and hurried down the steps, then ran toward the barn. "Mama, there's a man here!" He disappeared inside, and after a few minutes, a young woman in jeans and rough boots, her blonde hair pulled back into a ponytail under her hat, came out of the barn holding the boy's hand.

"What can I do for you?" she asked skeptically.

"I'm your new neighbor, Brantley Calderone. I moved in next door a week ago. I wanted to stop by and say hello." He wished he'd brought something along with him. He seemed sort of stupid standing there empty-handed.

"Nathan, go on and pick up your toys and put them away like I told you earlier. Your daddy is not going to be happy if you leave them everywhere." She waited until he was gone and then stepped a little closer. "The same neighbor where Renae was killed yesterday?"

"Yes. I came home and found her on my porch. It's so sad. She was very helpful and seemed kind."

"Renae was a bitch from hell," she hissed. "She didn't deserve to be killed, though. May she be tormented forever."

"I take it you weren't friends, Mrs....?"

"Julie Beltz, and you met my son, Nathan." She turned to him hesitantly. "My husband will be home in just a few minutes. So don't try anything."

"I'm only trying to be neighborly. I didn't hurt Renae, and I certainly wouldn't hurt anyone else. But I suppose it's a little much to ask you to believe me."

"It's all over town where Renae was killed, and folks are putting two and two together." She glared at him.

"I wasn't even home when she was killed." God, he should have thought about this. "Maybe I should go. I didn't mean to bother you." Brantley turned and walked back to his truck.

"Brantley," she called from behind him, and he stopped and turned to face her. "It will be easy enough to find out if you done it."

"I was at the store when it happened, and I tried to help her." Brantley knew it was going to be impossible to convince anyone he

24

hadn't hurt Renae. "I'm sorry to have bothered you." He tipped his hat the way Mack had earlier and then pulled open his truck door.

"Shit," she said. "This town can't get anything right, no matter what." Julie walked up behind him, and Brantley slowly turned around. "Anyone can see you don't have it in you to shoot anyone." Her mouth turned up in a slight smile. "How did you know Renae, anyway? Was she after you?"

"After me?" Brantley asked.

"That woman went after every man in town. Married or not, didn't matter. She didn't want a husband of her own—she just wanted everyone else's." She yanked her hat off her head and fanned herself with it. "I got some ice tea. Why don't you sit on the porch, and I'll get you a glass?" She stomped toward the house, and Brantley closed his truck door.

He followed her to the porch and sat down while she went inside. Nathan hurried through the yard, picking up toys and carrying them back into the house, running by every few minutes.

"They go in the toy box. Not on the living room floor," Julie called, and Brantley smiled at Nathan's groan. Nathan stayed inside for a few more minutes and then burst out of the door to go gather more toys. Julie came out with three glasses, two ice tea and one that looked like lemonade.

"Thank you," Brantley said when she handed him a glass.

"Nathan, when you're done with the other toys, you can ride your bicycle in the driveway, and I have some lemonade for you."

He hurried up to her, drank part of the glass, handed it back, and then set about racing to finish what he'd started.

"He never stands still for two minutes. Sometimes I wish I could bottle his energy."

Brantley nodded. "Why did you invite me to stay?"

"Because I trust Mack, and if he thought you were guilty, he'd have arrested you and taken the heat. Unfortunately, there are people in this town who aren't so logical. Besides, you haven't been in town long enough to hate her the way half the women do."

"Only half?" Brantley asked.

"Yeah. The other half are either too young or have husbands that are too old. Renae's husband—well, ex-husband—is a real piece of work. Drank too much. Still does, I hear. When she left him, I guess she thought she was free and made the most of it." Julie drank from her glass, watched Nathan, and then turned back to him. "So why did you buy the Richardson place?" She looked him over head to toe. "You don't seem like the type to want to run a ranch on your own." She chuckled. "Where did you get those boots?"

"Before I left New York." He shifted his gaze downward. "What's wrong with them?"

"They look like you're going to some club. They'll never hold up to any sort of hard work. And your hat is for show too. Not that it's any of my business."

Brantley bristled until he realized she hadn't meant anything by it other than an observation.

"Is Daddy coming home?" Nathan asked as he bounded up on the porch and gulped from the glass of lemonade Julie offered him.

"Not for a while. But he'd be so proud that you cleaned up your toys." She hugged Nathan to her as he whimpered. "I'm sorry, sweetheart. He called a few minutes ago." She sounded just as disappointed as Nathan looked. "He still has a week, but he said he'd call you tonight. If you're good, I'll take you out on your pony this afternoon." She glanced at Brantley as if apologizing for her earlier lie.

Brantley sipped his tea and watched as a sheriff's department vehicle pulled into the drive. Mack got out of the car, and Nathan handed his mother his glass and rushed off the porch.

"Sheriff Mack."

"Nathan," Mack said. He hugged the boy and then walked him back to the porch. "It looks like you have a visitor."

"Yes." Nathan turned to him and stared, putting a finger to his lips as he thought.

"That's Mr. Brantley," Mack said as they climbed the steps. "I was just checking that you were doing all right."

26

"We're fine, and you know it isn't necessary." Julie turned to Brantley. "My husband is in the Army Reserves, and he was supposed to be done with his annual training, but they wanted him to stay a week longer. Nathan is really missing his daddy. Mack stops in to see how we are."

"Denny and I went to school together," Mack told him.

"Brantley came over to say hello and meet his neighbors," Julie explained.

"He just left my place," Brantley said, looking at Mack.

"Yeah. I was headed here and got a call, but it was cancelled, so I decided to visit anyway." Mack nodded. "Meeting the neighbors is good."

"He and I already talked about what happened yesterday," Julie said.

"And he seems to have not had a hand in any of that," Mack confirmed.

"I didn't think he had," Julie said. "There are plenty of people in town who didn't like her."

"Now, Julie. Just because the two of you never saw eye to eye doesn't mean that everyone in town was out to get her. She was a hard-driving businesswoman."

"I know. If she were a man, none of us would think twice, but because she was a woman...." Julie stood and walked to the door. "I still say she was a bitch and that's the end of it."

"Mama, bad word," Nathan scolded.

"Sorry, sweetheart," Julie said just before the screen door slammed closed. Brantley watched her go and wondered if something was wrong. Julie returned quickly with a pitcher of tea and another glass. "Go and ride your bike," Julie told Nathan, and he jumped off the porch, then climbed onto the small blue bike with training wheels. "You getting any closer to finding who whacked Renae?" She poured Mack some tea and refilled Brantley's glass.

"We're making progress," he said but offered nothing more.

"You know this whole thing has tongues wagging all over town," Julie said.

Brantley figured she left off the part about how he was being blamed because he was sitting right there.

"Yes, I know. I've fielded calls from a number of people, including the mayor." Mack looked tired. "When something like this happens, everyone wants answers, and they don't care if the guilty party is caught, just that someone is punished."

"Great." Going back to New York was looking better and better all the time. "I came here because I wanted a different life, open spaces where I could breathe, maybe put down roots. I didn't expect to become a pariah immediately. That usually takes a little while." Brantley tried to lighten things up, but it wasn't helping.

"Look at me, Mama," Nathan yelled.

"That's great, honey. Don't go near the road," Julie said. "He misses his dad pretty badly. They do a lot together, and I've been so busy with Denny gone that I haven't had as much time to spend with him as I should." She drank the rest of her tea, and Brantley finished his glass.

"Thank you so much for the tea and the conversation. I really appreciate it, and it was so nice to meet you."

"You too." Julie stood, and they shook hands before Brantley went to his truck. "I'll see you later."

"Nathan, come up here, sweetheart, so Mr. Brantley can go."

Brantley watched as Nathan raced up on his bike and stopped near the porch steps. Julie held the bike, and Brantley waved before backing down the drive and returning the way he'd come. The visit had proved somewhat enlightening. It was clear that Julie didn't like Renae, but Brantley doubted she'd shot her either. Still, it was nice to have met Julie and maybe begun a friendship.

As he reached his drive, Brantley figured he'd pressed his luck enough for one day and decided not to visit any more neighbors. He turned in and pulled up near the house. He got out as a police vehicle parked next to his truck.

"Is there something you need, Mack?"

"Not particularly. I just wanted to tell you that I will make it clear in town that you are not a suspect in Renae's murder.

Some people will believe it and others will stick to their stubborn ignorance, but it should lower some of the barriers to getting to know people."

"Thanks, but I think yesterday made that process doubly hard. What people are going to remember is that she was murdered at my house, so therefore I must have had something to do with it."

"I'll catch the real killer, and then that will put an end to all this." Mack came around to where he was standing. "I was wondering if you have plans for dinner."

"Just heating something up."

"Then how about coming into town with me? We could go to the diner. It's where everyone meets. If people see you eating with the sheriff, they'll know you aren't a threat because I don't usually eat with criminal suspects."

"You don't have to go out of your way just to be nice. I'll figure out a way through this." He was a New Yorker, after all. He could do anything if he put his mind to it.

"Suit yourself. I figured you'd need to eat and might be getting tired of your own cooking." Mack cocked his eyebrow just so. It was both hot and disarming.

"I'd like to get some dinner. Do you want to meet in town?"

Mack's radio sounded. He answered the call and returned his attention to Brantley. "That would be great. Meet you at the diner at six." Mack turned back toward his car but stopped before he opened the door. "One word of advice. Wear what you're comfortable in."

"Why does everyone seem to comment on my clothes?" Brantley asked. They were supposed to be the latest style in this sort of thing.

"Because they aren't you." Mack tilted his hat, climbed in his cruiser, and began to pull out of the drive, but stopped. "Don't forget to call if the cattle aren't moved," he yelled out his window, and Brantley waved his hat, keeping it in his hand when he was done.

Once Mack was gone, Brantley went inside, tossed his hat on one of the chairs, and wandered through to the kitchen. He got some water and peered out the window. There were just a few of the dark shapes toward the one side of the field, with men on ATVs around them. Andy was moving his cattle as promised. At least that bit of excitement was over.

Brantley made a light lunch and ate it in front of the television. Afterward he ended up dozing on the sofa for a little while. When he woke, he wasn't sure what the hell to do. He was bored stiff. People in the West always seemed so busy in the movies. There were always things to get done and never enough time to do everything. It hadn't occurred to Brantley that he'd have nothing to do and enough time on his hands that he'd want to wring his own neck. In a week he'd unpacked everything and done the little chores around the house. Maybe he could explore and clean out the barn. He hoped to have animals to fill it at some point, but he needed to find people to help with that. But the chances of finding good people had probably died along with Renae. Who would want to work on a ranch where someone had been murdered? This whole situation sucked.

HE WAS a mess. Brantley had spent the afternoon cleaning out the barn. He'd shoveled old dirt and God knows what else into a wheelbarrow he'd had to repair before he could fill it and carry it away. He'd been lucky. When he decided to start this little chore, he'd realized he didn't have any tools, but someone had left a few things in the old tack room, so he was able to scoop away the junk and sweep out the loft and main floor. So at the moment, the place was really clean and he was completely filthy.

Brantley put away his tools, checked his watch, and hurried into the house. He needed to shower and dress fast or he was going to be late for dinner.

He very nearly was. It took plenty of rushing, but he pulled through the small town and parked in front of the diner with two minutes to spare. He didn't know what Mack drove when he was off duty, so he wasn't sure if he had arrived yet. Brantley went into the diner and stood near the hostess station as the entire place went quiet. He swallowed, all eyes on him, but soon people began talking once again. He had no doubt that he—and the speculation about whether he'd killed Renae—was the topic of conversation.

"Excuse me," a large man said as he ambled to where Brantley was standing. "How can you show your face here? You should be in jail." He parted his lips and showed a set of broken teeth. Brantley figured he'd lost them in bar fights or something.

"That's enough, Cal," Mack said from behind him.

Brantley was getting to know that voice very well, and he had never been so pleased to hear it in his life.

"Sheriff... he...," Cal began.

"Mr. Calderone is here to have dinner with me," Mack said, and the wind went out of Cal's sails in the blink of an eye.

"But...."

"Mr. Calderone was in town at the time Renae was killed, and there are witnesses to support that. So back off." Mack stepped closer and stood his ground. "People are innocent until proven guilty. That's how the law works, and you don't get to use that pea brain of yours to think anything different. Now go on back to your dinner." He pointed, and Cal turned on his heels and sat back down.

"Thanks."

Mack nodded and led the way to an empty table. "This is a seat-yourself kind of place. Marlene only seats people on Saturday when it seems like the whole town comes here for dinner."

"I wasn't expecting the welcome wagon, but...," he began.

"Cal is as dumb as a box of rocks, and he always acts before he thinks." Mack turned to the huge man, exchanging glares. Mack waited until Cal looked away, and then he turned back around. "Most people just want something to talk about, and someone getting killed is the story of the year around here."

"I suppose. I just wish someone else was at the center of the story."

"Word will get around fast that you didn't do it, and then they will start speculating about who did. It's the nature of a small town." Mack leaned over the table. "And sometimes the mill conjures up a nugget of truth that can actually be helpful."

31

"Okay." Brantley stopped when their server, a girl from the high school by the look of her, approached their table.

"Mandy, how are you?" Mack said. "This is Brantley Calderone. He's new in town."

She turned to him warily. "What can I get you? The meatloaf is real good, and so is the pot pie."

"I'll have the pot pie," Brantley said.

"Me too. With a coffee and a salad," Mack said.

"That sounds good," Brantley added, and Mandy flashed Mack a smile before leaving the table. "Do you know everyone in town? After what happened, I wanted to get an alarm for the house. I ordered a basic setup, but I need some help installing it."

"I grew up here, and I know some people who can help with that. Everyone in this town is connected somehow. My mother was Lakota Sioux, and my father is Andy's cousin. The hothead you met earlier. We were the poor relations. Dad worked cattle, and Mom, well, she didn't stick around too long after I was born. Dad fell in love with her, they got married and had me, but Dad said he wasn't what she needed. I was two when Mom took off. She was in a bad space and really unhappy." Mack must have realized he'd gotten off track. "I'll get someone to help with the installation."

"Thanks." Then Brantley returned to the previous topic. "Did she return to the reservation?"

"Yes, but she took her own life just a few weeks later. Her brother called my dad and told him. That's why I wear my hair longer, in honor of her."

"Is your dad still alive?"

"Yeah." Mack smiled. "He's in a wheelchair now, but not much stops him."

Brantley did some figuring in his head. "Your dad can't be that old."

"He's not. He got thrown and stepped on by a horse a little over a year ago. It injured his back so he can't use his legs any longer. Dad lives with me, and the neighbors watch out for him when I'm not there. Right now he's trying to figure out something he can do to make some extra money. Lord knows what he'll come up with." Mack's indulgent smile told Brantley that the two of them cared very much for each other. "I'll take you to meet him sometime. Dad loves talking to new folks."

Mandy brought their drinks and made a hasty retreat. Brantley did his best to ignore it.

"So why law enforcement?" he asked as he added a little sugar to the strong coffee.

"After college, I joined the force in Sioux Falls, and I intended to move to a larger city and join a large department once I got some experience. I was in Sioux Falls for about five years. But after Dad's accident, I moved here and joined the sheriff's department, and then ran for sheriff when the last one got embroiled in a scandal and had to step down." Mack sipped from his mug, and Brantley watched him, a familiar flutter kicking up in his stomach. He knew what that meant. He'd been admiring Mack for the last couple days, but now that he got to talk to him, he realized the looks Mack was giving him every now and then weren't because he was waiting for Brantley to reveal something about the case. They indicated interest, or at least they seemed to.

Brantley had figured he'd have to give up on any kind of relationship once he moved out here, and that had been more than fine. They always ended in disaster anyway, so why bother? His goal had been to build a new life, one closer to the land. He blinked a few times, chastising himself for being ridiculous. He had to be reading the signals wrong.

Their food arrived, and Brantley arranged the plates, figuring he'd eat the hot food first. Moving his salad bowl knocked his fork on the floor, and as he bent down to pick it up, the window next to him exploded.

CHAPTER 3

"EVERYONE GET down and stay there," Mack called. "Quiet down and stay low." He needed to hear and waited to see if there were going to be any more shots. His main concern was keeping everyone safe. Keeping his head down, he made his way to the door and peered out across the street. He saw nothing.

"Mandy," he said turning to where she was huddled near the counter. "Call the police and tell them I'm already here and want backup now."

She hurried behind the counter, and a few seconds later, Mack heard her on the phone.

"It had to have come from the roof across the street," Brantley said.

Mack turned, scowling at Brantley for following him and impressed the guy wasn't cowering in fear. "How do you know?"

"Angle of the shot," Brantley answered with a quaver in his voice that only managed to piss Mack off. "Are they still out there?"

"I doubt it. My guess is that they took one shot and took off."

Sirens sounded and vehicles pulled up in front of the diner. Mack continued staying low. "Zeb, it probably came from the roof across the street," he yelled when he saw Zeb get out and stay low behind his car.

Zeb got back in the car and took off before Mack could tell him to be careful. Thankfully no further shots rang out, and Zeb returned. "There's no one there. Whoever it was got away. But they left shells this time."

"Okay. Let's get everyone out of here and safely to their cars. Have folks come back to settle any bills." Mack turned to the owner, Marlene, who was in her midfifties and had seen just about everything. "Do you need us to get someone to board up the window?"

"Henry can do it," she said.

"Okay. Then let's get everyone out of here safely, and then we can figure out what the hell happened." He stood and carefully began helping people out around the mess and to their cars. It took a while, but they spoke to each of the patrons to find out what they'd seen and then got them on their way home. Then he went to work trying to piece everything together.

Leaving Brantley in the far booth, Mack retrieved the bullet and added it to evidence. At least this time they had both bullet and shell.

"It looks like it's from a hunting rifle," Zeb said.

"Like there aren't a million of those in the county," Mack grumbled. At least if they found a suspect rifle, they could try to match fired shells. "Marlene, you can sweep up if you want, and Henry can board up the window." They had taken pictures of everything, and Mack had gotten all he was going to from the scene.

"What's happening in this town?" Marlene asked. "A murder and now a shooting through my window that could have hurt anyone." Her frustration matched Mack's. "I know this isn't your fault, but you got to get to the bottom of this. It's going to be hell getting people back in here after this." She turned and began cleaning up, whisking her broom across the floor with much more force than was necessary. "Once you catch the son of a bitch who did this, I'd like to get the first shot at him. Maybe a load of buckshot in the ass will teach him a lesson."

Mack wasn't so sure of that. This guy was either on some sort of mission or had decided someone in this town had done him wrong and was going to try to get even. Mack had to get in this guy's head somehow and figure out what the hell he wanted. It was the only way to get to the bottom of this.

"Do you think this shooting was related to Renae's murder?" Brantley asked when Mack approached where he was huddled in the booth away from the windows.

"I don't know. But my gut is telling me it is."

"Sheriff," Zeb said as he hurried back into the diner. "You need to come see this."

Mack turned to leave, and Brantley followed closely behind him.

35

"Do you think I can go home now?" Brantley asked.

"Um. That's the problem," Zeb explained. "A number of people said they thought they heard two shots, but only one shattered the window."

"Did you find another one?" Mack asked, and Zeb pointed across the parking lot to Brantley's shiny new truck, which now had a shattered back window.

"The bullet went in the back window and shattered parts of the dash. We're going to have to haul it in to the station to get more light so we can dig the thing out. But it ripped up the insides good."

"Can we drive it over slowly?" Mack asked. "It's only a block."

"There's enough damage that it could short out the entire electrical system. A tow truck is best to move it."

"Okay. Call a truck and haul it to the station. Then get to work extricating the bullet. I'm going to take Brantley home." When it rained, it fucking poured. At least this show of violence left little doubt as to who the target of the attack had been. Mack had initially been afraid that it might be him, but this clearly singled out Brantley.

It was going to be a long night.

Mack walked to his car and waited for Brantley to get in the passenger seat. "Is there anyone who'll be with you at home?"

"It's just me," Brantley answered softly, worry and fear clear in his voice.

"Then I'm going to take you to my place. You shouldn't be alone, and certainly not way out there. Whoever the hell is behind this knows your movements and will be aware that you're on your own." Mack started the car and pulled out of the parking lot. He drove a few blocks and pulled into his drive.

The lights were on inside, casting rectangular squares across the lawn. "You'll be safe here, with other people around." Mack cut the engine and got out, scanning the surroundings before walking to the house. He opened the door, and the herd surged past him, circling Brantley, sniffing, and yipping. "It's all right. They're only interested in seeing if you have any treats. The lab is Leo, and the beagle is

Rex, and this one is Lulu." Mack picked up the poodle mix, and she squirmed with excitement in his arms. "They're all attention sluts." He motioned inside. "Come on in and they'll follow."

Brantley looked overwhelmed. "I've never had dogs."

"Why not?" Mack asked as he waited for Brantley to pass by and then closed the door.

"I lived in the city. A lot of people did, but I thought it unfair. Dogs need room, and being stuck in an apartment isn't fair. At least I didn't think so."

Mack nodded, then called, "Dad!"

The bathroom door opened, and his father rolled out and down the hall into the living room. "Heard there was some excitement at the diner."

Mack put Lulu back on her feet. "Yeah. Dad, this is Brantley Calderone. He's new in town. His truck was shot up, along with the diner window, so he's going to be in the guest room for tonight."

"It's good to meet you," Mack's dad said, shaking hands with Brantley. "Call me Lew." He turned back to Mack. "You need to go back to the station?" he asked, and Mack nodded.

"I have a lot of work to do to try to get to the bottom of this whole mess." Mack rubbed the back of his neck. "Don't wait up for me. I'll probably be really late." Mack turned to Brantley. "Dad will look after you, and so will these guys." Time was of the essence, and he needed to get to work.

Mack strode to the door and stopped with his hand on the doorknob. Brantley looked so alone, even with Lulu jumping around his legs. Mack had never thought about having a boyfriend again or allowing anyone into his life. Not seriously since coming back. But Brantley tugged at his heart. Fucking hell if Mack could figure out why. Maybe it was the fear in his huge blue eyes, or it could be the fact that even though he was scared, Brantley still held an inner confidence and strength that most men would have lost after all the excitement of the last couple of days. One thing was for sure: Mack wanted Brantley to be safe regardless of whether it was his job or not. That was important.

37

For a brief second, Brantley's gaze caught his, and they shared a moment of connection that Mack felt to his gut. Mack's belly tingled with the familiar call of interest, and then Brantley turned away.

Mack pulled open the door so he could hurry back to work.

MACK DRAGGED himself home hours later. They had gotten exactly nowhere in the investigation. The bullet had been recovered from Brantley's truck, but the thing was a mess. The impact had done a number on it. Still, the shooter hadn't actually hurt anyone… this time.

He opened the door and went in softly, expecting the herd to group around his legs. Nothing happened. The house was quiet. His dad sat in his favorite recliner with a blanket, head resting back, eyes closed.

"Do you want me to help you to bed?" Mack asked. His dad often slept in his chair when he was worried.

"In a minute. I talked to that young man for a while. He's something else. Got guts, that one."

"How so?"

"There are lots of kinds of courage. You have it under fire. He spent the evening talking to me and advising me on what kinds of investments I should make, put together a whole plan and where the money should be, and then when I should change it and what to. The guy is really smart. At some point a car went by—you know that old clunker Mrs. Abbott drives? Makes a god-awful noise. He tensed but then went right back to work. Nerves steady as anything. Sometimes going on after an incident like that without falling apart is real courage."

"I like him too, Dad," Mack said to his own surprise. "Now let's get you in your chair and to bed." Mack watched to make sure his dad didn't need help getting to the chair and then quietly wheeled him down to his room. His dad went inside and closed the door.

Mack turned to go to his own room but stopped outside the partially open guest room door. He peered inside. There was little light, but a soft snore reached his ears. He knew that was Lulu. That little girl could wake the dead sometimes. She was curled next to Brantley's legs, with Rex on the other side. They raised their heads and then put them down once again. Leo didn't even do that. Mack's dogs seem to have fallen in love with Brantley, or if nothing else, they knew he needed them. "Night, guys," Mack whispered.

"Mack?" Brantley asked sleepily and shifted, the bed squeaking slightly. Mack had meant to fix that. One of the million things he needed to do when he got around to it.

"I just got back. Go back to sleep."

Brantley sat up, and Mack stepped back. "Did you find out anything?"

"Very little. The guy is a ghost. He seemed to leave little behind besides bullets. No one saw anything. They only heard the shots." He stepped away from the doorway to go to his room when Brantley got out of bed. Mack forced his attention to the shine of his brass doorknob. He needed to look anywhere other than at the skin hinted at by the flash of gold. "He just disappeared."

"He can't have."

"I have people watching the building where he took the shot, and we'll go over when it gets light and see if there's anything we missed." Mack let go of the knob and turned around.

Brantley stood framed in the doorway, the hall light highlighting his golden skin. He was lean, svelte, and maybe a little pale from years indoors. Mack stopped his head from tilting forward to follow the line of his hips down into the sweats that his dad must have lent him from his drawer. They were a little big on Brantley, and damn it, he'd done exactly what he'd said he wasn't going to do. He couldn't help it. Heat welled up inside, and he swallowed hard to help wet the inside of his mouth once again.

"But you will catch him?" Brantley asked.

Lulu padded out into the hallway, looking up at Brantley as if to ask why he was crazy enough to be up at this hour, and then she ambled toward the living room.

"I will. But this is turning into a bigger puzzle than I expected." And he was so damned tired, he could hardly think. His attention kept being drawn to Brantley, and what sent heat shooting through him was that Brantley was looking back.

"I'm good at puzzles and things," Brantley said. "That's what decoding the financial data I dealt with involved. Every company and industry was a puzzle. They had things that were at their center, nuggets of information that would yield amazing results."

"Well, I'm just a law enforcement officer, and this one is stumping me. Whoever is doing this seems to be going after you." Damn, Mack wanted to go after him, but in a very different way. He stepped closer, and Brantley stayed in place. This was not a good idea, and yet he was drawn to Brantley like a magnet. It had been quite a while since he'd been involved with anyone, and even then he hadn't felt this kind of pull. But Brantley was involved in a case, a police matter. It was likely he was the intended victim, and Mack had brought him home in order to provide a safe place for him, and that meant a place safe *from* him too. "Do you need anything?" he managed to croak.

"I was going to get some water."

"Come on." Mack led him to the kitchen. "I have juice and tea if you want that."

"No caffeine," Brantley said as he sat at the kitchen table.

Mack got two glasses, poured orange juice into each one, and took a seat across from Brantley. "I will find this guy," Mack said. "I hate unsolved cases, and I haven't had any since I came into office. The people here aren't going to reelect me if I don't do my job. And this is as high profile as it gets."

"It's my life they're after."

"I know that. I'm only saying that we have the same goal, and I take pride in solving my cases. I will do everything I can. You have to know that." Mack downed his juice as though it were a huge shot of gin.

Lulu came in, and Brantley bent down and picked her up.

"I see you've made a number of friends."

"I think so. They've all been friendly."

"They love attention, and I'm not home enough."

Lulu squirmed, so Brantley put her down again. She ambled over, and Mack picked her up. She settled on his lap and put her head down. He stroked her fur and tried to relax. It was difficult with Brantley sitting near him, half-naked, pulling him toward his heat. He wanted to give in but resisted.

"Does the town know... about you?" Brantley asked. "I see the way you look at me." Brantley broke the gaze Mack hadn't even known they were sharing, and then his skin rippled with a chill at the loss.

"I don't know," Mack answered. "I'm an honest person and I don't lie, so I never told anyone I was... straight, I guess. But I never told anyone otherwise either. In this town I've never had occasion to. After I returned, I went to work, and I take care of Dad. There hasn't been anyone who caught my interest, so the subject never really came up." Mack had never been the kind of guy who ran on at the mouth, but he wanted Brantley. Damn, why did he always wish for what he couldn't have?

"I didn't mean to impugn your character." Brantley drank half his juice, and Mack wished a drop, just one, would escape and caress its way down Brantley's neck and chest. Then Mack would have an excuse to chase it with his finger. "In New York, I was out but hermetic. My work took most of my time, and I never had luck with men. They'd be interested at first, but almost every time it was because of my bank account." Brantley sighed. "I had one boyfriend, Johnny, who, after dating me a month, wanted me to invest his money for him and make him rich. He thought I had some golden touch that would turn his few thousand dollars into millions overnight." Brantley finished his juice and put down the glass. "He left me shortly after I turned him down." He got up and took his glass to the sink. "All I wanted when I came here was a simpler life. I didn't want all the stress and hustle of the city. I hoped to have a place, maybe get some horses so I could learn to ride. I dreamed of that as a kid. More than anything I wanted a pony, but there was no place to put a pony in a Manhattan apartment.

I thought I'd build up the ranch, knowing I'd have to hire people, and then maybe I could have a business."

"What about someone to share it with?" Mack asked.

"I didn't think about that. If I couldn't find someone in New York, I figured that sort of thing was out of the question anyway, so I didn't give it much consideration."

"You should," Mack said, watching Brantley's back as he heaved in a breath.

"What I need to do is go to bed." Brantley turned from the sink to face him. "This is… everything is…."

Mack drew himself to his feet without thought, gliding toward Brantley without lifting his feet. At least he didn't feel them lift. All he felt and saw was Brantley getting closer. Brantley backed up against the sink, and Mack stopped, giving Brantley an out. He wouldn't force anyone, but his entire being throbbed and urged him forward. "You should go now if that's what you want to do," Mack breathed.

"I know I should, but I don't think I can." Brantley raised a hand, and Mack caught it and brought them together in a first touch that promised more.

Brantley stepped forward and leaned in closer, tightening his hold on Mack's hand as if he thought he would bolt. Their gazes probed deeply, each looking inside the other for what he needed most. Brantley pressed forward as he inhaled, and Mack tugged him still closer.

The fluorescent light over their heads buzzed softly as Brantley closed the distance between them. Chest to chest, he pushed Mack back until the counter pressed lightly into Mack's lower back. Brantley's musky scent, heavy with sleep and arousal, swirled into Mack's nose, intensifying as Brantley got even closer. Mack's lips parted, and he tilted his head to the side, preparing for what he hoped like hell was coming next. He was afraid to blink for fear it would break the connection between them and Brantley would change his mind and decide that now would be a good time to go to his room.

Mack released his grip and slid his hands around Brantley's waist, tugging him in even closer and slipping his fingers under the waistband of Brantley's sweatpants, the smooth warm skin teasing him even more. He wanted it all, and he wanted everything right the hell now. His pants were too damn tight, and he needed some relief, and the most damning thing of all was that he hadn't even gotten a first taste of Brantley and he was already ready for seconds.

He closed the gap between them, taking Brantley's lips in a bruising kiss. Mack hadn't meant to be that intense right out of the gate, but his control was slipping. Thankfully Brantley met his intensity measure for measure, sliding his tongue along Mack's in what was less of a duel and more of the two of them pulled by the same internal need that neither seemed able to control. Mack tasted the tang of orange juice still on Brantley's lips, but that didn't last for long. Soon the rich earthiness of Brantley came through, and Mack was hooked and wanted more.

Light-headed on Brantley's musk, he pulled him closer, the heat of Brantley's chest radiating through his shirt as Mack memorized the contours of Brantley's smooth back. "God, I want you," Mack whispered when they moved apart just enough that Mack still felt the heat from Brantley's lips. He dared to let his hands roam lower, sliding over the fabric to cup Brantley's firm, bubble-shaped ass.

"I…. It's your house… your dad is home…." Brantley sputtered even as he cut himself off with another kiss. If that was how Brantley reacted to passion, Mack could grow to crave those mutters of incoherence.

He could feel the sweatpants riding low on Brantley's hips. It would be easy to push them past the rod of steel that pressed into Mack's hip and take what he wanted. Brantley was certainly willing, and if the growls from deep in his throat weren't an indication of what he wanted, the rising heat from his skin was certainly more than enough of a welcome.

"Mack…. I…."

"Fuck, you taste like heaven," Mack muttered, letting his hands rove around to Brantley's chest, about to test whether his nipples were as sensitive as the rest of Brantley seemed to be.

A howl went up from the guest room, followed by barks and the racing of paws and clicking of nails on the floor, running past the kitchen toward the front door. Leo growled as he stood at attention by the door. Rex bounded up into the chair, howling, head tilted upward, while Lulu added her own alarm.

"What is it?" Mack asked as he approached the front window. He parted the curtains and grabbed his gun while working the door open. "Brantley, hold the dogs inside."

Brantley raced over, lifted Lulu into his arms, and held Rex's collar.

Mack pushed Leo out of the way and stepped out into the night in time to see a lone figure racing down the street in dark clothes. Mack flipped on the outside lights and let the door close silently after him.

The only sounds that reached his ears now were the chirp of the insects and the hum of an occasional car engine from the next street. Other than that, the night was silent.

Mack thought about going after the guy, but there was little use. He went back inside, leaving the outdoor lights on, and closed the door. He wasn't sure what to think at this point. "It's all right, guys, you did good." Mack stroked all three dogs, and now that it was once again quiet, they settled down.

"Mack," his father called.

"It's fine, Dad. Go back to sleep." Mack tried to stifle a yawn and failed. It was way past time to get some sleep. He put his gun away and yawned widely again.

"I'll see you in the morning." Brantley turned back toward the hall that led to the bedrooms.

Rex and Leo looked at him and then turned to Mack before trotting off after Brantley.

Mack wanted to be upset, but the truth was, it would be nice to have some room in his own bed for one night, and Brantley seemed to need them. The dogs always knew. He set Lulu down, and she sat, looking up at him. Mack locked all the doors, then went down the hallway to his room.

Temptation slept right across the hall, but Brantley had made his choice, and Mack would abide by it. Lulu followed him into his room, jumped up onto the bed, and lay down right in the exact middle. Mack went to his bathroom and cleaned up before undressing and climbing under the covers. "Move over, you little bed pig," Mack growled, and Lulu did the same right back before shifting over, and they settled in.

MORNING CAME way too early, but thankfully the rest of the night was quiet, and he got a few hours' sleep before dragging himself out of bed, dressing, and leaving the house. He was barely awake when he met Zeb and his other deputy, Ronnie Carvey, at the building across from the diner. "Spread out and look around. This guy couldn't have left without any trace at all. He dropped his shells and left them, so he can make a mistake, and we need to see what else he did."

Mack stood at the base of the building, looking up, wondering how in the hell the guy had gotten up there. Had he carried his own ladder? "Zeb? How did you get up there last night?"

"The dumpster was right up against the building."

"So it was moved. Who did that? Find out from the guys who were here last night."

"I moved it after I got back down. I didn't want anyone else up there," Zeb explained. "I used gloves, and I'm glad I did. That thing is nasty, and it smells to high heaven. Think when we're done we can get them to hose it down or something?"

"Let's keep our eyes on the prize, all right? Let's go over what we know. He arrived from somewhere and most likely had a car or truck parked back here."

"There was an empty space right here," Zeb said and paced off the area. "The rest of this was parked up. So it makes sense he parked here and went up to the roof."

"Why?" Mack asked, not expecting an answer.

"If the shooter was after the new guy, then he had to have followed him to know where he was," Ronnie said. "I'm assuming the shot wasn't random."

45

"It wasn't," Mack said as he continued looking around. "Get a ladder so we can go up and see what we have." He continued scouring the area, trying to visualize what happened here. This exercise was a long shot, but they had to get any evidence they could from the scene, and Mack was not happy this guy was pulling all this off under his nose.

Zeb returned five minutes later with a ladder, probably borrowed from one of the merchants, and Mack climbed to the roof and motioned Zeb to come up with him. He stepped carefully, easily finding the evidence markings where the casings had been. Mack had a good view of the diner. "He must have used a scope. You can see the diner, but you'd need more detail if you wanted to take a precision shot."

"Do you think this guy is a sniper?" Zeb asked.

"Not necessarily. A hunter with a good rifle could have made this shot. But it's a good bet there's some training involved." Mack knew that was a supposition and not even a strong one. Once again, what he had was a whole lot of nothing. Mack went back to the ladder and climbed down. "Let's go back to the station." He needed to go over everything he had again and see if there was some nugget of information that he'd missed.

"DID YOU find anything?" Brantley asked when Mack returned home that night, and Mack had to tell him no. The entire day had been nearly useless, and he was not an inch closer to finding out who was behind this.

"I was able to arrange for someone to fix your truck for you. It's going to take some time because they really messed up the electrical wiring."

"It's all right. I called my insurance company, and they said to take care of it," Brantley said. "I was hoping someone could take me back out to the ranch."

"You can't stay there," Mack said. "You're being watched, or at least you were last night. Otherwise how would anyone know you were at the diner? So I'll be glad to take you out there to get anything you need and check on the place, but I want you to stay here. You'll be safer—right, Dad?" Mack asked.

"Yeah, boy. You need to keep safe, and the best way to do that is to let Mack try to protect you."

"I don't want to be a bother."

"And I don't want this asshole to succeed and kill you," Mack said.

Brantley turned to him. "I don't think that's his goal. I've had tons of time to think about it today, and if he wanted to kill me, he had the chance to do it. He killed Renae from not much closer than he was last night. That is, assuming this is the same guy. And I'm betting it is."

"That makes sense."

"So the real question is, what does he want? If he wasn't out to kill me last night, then what sort of message was he sending or what did he hope to accomplish? I'm willing to bet that he's trying to scare me off. He was after me, there's no doubt, and he shot up my truck and no one else's. The shot through the restaurant window came near my head. He had a clear enough shot to hit me, but didn't."

"Okay. If that's true, then why? What could they want?"

"The easiest answer is the ranch. The land. I have water and some of my neighbors don't," Brantley said.

"You're thinking Andy, aren't you?" Mack said.

"I know he's your cousin and that you'd probably not want to think of him that way, but yeah. He's kind of a dick, he needs the water that I have, and if I'm gone, he could let his cattle graze there until someone else either bought the property, or I can see him trying to take it off my hands so I could leave."

"We don't have any proof," Mack reminded him.

"Nope," Brantley agreed and remained quiet.

"Son, why don't you take him to the ranch so he can get some of his things? I'm sure Brantley would also like to check that everything is okay out there as well. Take Leo and Rex. They'd like a good run, and you know they'll sound the alarm if necessary."

"All right." He scooped up Lulu, placed her on his father's lap, and then called the other two, who barreled out as soon as he asked if they wanted to go for a ride. "Would you take them out to the truck? I need to change. I'll be out in two minutes." Mack hurried to his room and changed in record time. Then he jogged outside and found Brantley sitting in the cab of his old truck, Leo in the back and Rex perched on Brantley's lap, tongue lolling, all waiting for him.

That was one hell of a sight. Brantley looked good in his truck. Hell, Mack figured Brantley would look good anywhere—in his truck, on his sofa, in his bed. He'd looked and felt amazing in his kitchen last night. Mack wanted a repeat of that, for sure, maybe with the addition of—nope, make that the removal of—a lot more clothing.

Mack pulled his thoughts away from how Brantley would look naked and got into the truck, started the powerful engine, and backed out of the drive.

"I keep wondering what I'm going to find," Brantley said, petting Rex as they went.

Mack had to admit he didn't know. If the incident in the middle of the night was an indication, then the shooter knew Brantley was at his house. Mack was going to have to be extra careful. "I think it will be fine. If they want the ranch, then it's likely they want it intact."

Brantley nodded, biting his lower lip.

Mack had tried to be reassuring, but he wasn't sure either. What if their shooter was getting frustrated and decided to escalate? Mack's experience told him that was the usual pattern with people who were willing to resort to violence to get what they wanted.

He made the turn out of town and picked up speed. There was little traffic, and Mack sped up along the country roads. He didn't exceed the speed limit by too much because he didn't want to set a bad example, but Brantley's anxiety filled the cab. The dogs felt it. Leo placed his head against Brantley's arm. Mack pressed the brake to slow down as he approached an intersection, and nothing happened. He pushed harder, but they didn't engage at all. "Shit, the brakes are gone." He downshifted into second, and the truck slowed. Mack hoped to hell no one was coming along the side street because he was not going to be able to stop in time. "Hang on to the dogs," he said and downshifted once again. The engine engaged, and the truck lurched as it slowed quickly, the engine screaming as it offered resistance and slowed them further.

The truck rolled through the intersection, and a car crossed just behind them. Brakes squealed, and Mack managed to pull the truck to the side of the road. As the truck rolled to a stop, Mack threw the gear into neutral and yanked the parking brake before jumping out. "Is everyone all right?" he yelled as he hurried to the other car.

"What the hell were you doing?" Taylor Hopper said as he got out of his car. "You nearly killed us." He turned toward him. "Sheriff?"

Mack's heart pounded in his ears, his mind screaming that he'd nearly hurt some of the people he'd sworn to protect. "Yes. My brakes failed completely. I wanted to make sure everyone was okay."

"We're fine. Shaken up, but fine."

His heart rate slowed a little. "Is Isaac in the car with you?"

Taylor nodded. "Anne, as well."

"But they're all okay?"

"Yes. We didn't collide. It only scared them. I saw you and managed to slow enough to miss, but it was pretty harrowing for a few seconds."

"I'm sorry about that." Mack peered into the window, apologizing to Anne and waving to Isaac in his car seat, the youngster waving back with one hand, the other thumb stuck in his mouth.

"Do you need help or a ride?" Taylor asked.

"I'll call in to get one. Thanks. We're a little full with the dogs." Mack stepped away, and Taylor got back in his car and slowly continued on his way. Mack pulled his phone out of his pocket and called in. "Gloria, I need a car out on Route 21 near Wilson. Send someone right away with sirens!"

"Right away," she said and hung up.

Mack walked back to his truck, opened the door, and got back inside. He lowered the windows for some air.

"Is someone on their way?" Brantley asked.

"You better believe it. I bet the son of a bitch cut my brake line last night." Mack smacked the steering wheel with his hand. "One of the deputies will be out here soon. I hope to God it's Zeb. He knows his way around cars a lot better than anyone else on the force." He should have been specific, but his men had been working a lot of hours, so if Zeb was off, he didn't want to bother him. Mack had a feeling that this case was going to occupy a lot of resources.

"I hope so." Brantley fidgeted in his seat. "I hope nothing has happened out at the ranch."

"Not to sound unfeeling, but if the worst happened, is there a lot that you couldn't replace?"

"There are pictures and things, but most of them are on my computer, and that's backed up." Brantley thought a few seconds. "It's my home. I know I've only been there a week, but it's still my home."

"I didn't mean to be callous. I understand the feelings associated with home." He also understood what it meant to feel like a victim, and this shooter was most definitely doing his best to drive that home. Mack certainly didn't want to add to it. "I'm sorry."

"Don't be. There are things in the house that I don't want to lose. Mainly the art, things like that. Everything is insured and all that, but I enjoy them, and it isn't as though I can just replace them. What are you thinking?"

"I don't know. I just don't want you to be hurt." He cleared his throat. "I never want any innocent person in my county to be hurt," he clarified to hide his growing feelings.

"Let's get there and see what's happened." Brantley held Rex closer, and the beagle licked a line up Brantley's face.

A siren sounded, getting louder by the second. Zeb pulled up behind him and got out. "What happened?"

"The brakes failed. I think the brake line was cut. There was just enough fluid to get me out of town and then they failed. I think it happened last night. Can you take a look and see if you can fix it enough to get back into town?"

Zeb popped the hood and peered inside. "That's what it was. But the brake fluid is gone. I'll call for a tow, and I can fix it back in town, no problem." He stepped back and closed the hood. After calling for a tow truck, they all piled in Zeb's cruiser and drove to Brantley's.

The ranch looked the same, but Mack was careful. "Let me check inside first. Hand me your keys." He got out and walked to the front door, then used Brantley's keys to unlock it. He went from room to room and found nothing and no one. He motioned for Brantley, who came with the dogs and Zeb.

Leo and Rex explored and eventually made themselves at home on Brantley's sofa.

"Do you need help?" Mack asked while looking at a painting on the wall.

"I'm fine. Give me a few minutes," Brantley said from the other room, and he came out a few minutes later. "That's my favorite," he said, standing close enough to where Mack was that Mack could feel the heat from his shoulder.

"I've seen that one before. Some of the guys had a print of it when I was in college. I always liked pop art, and Warhol was a favorite." Mack leaned closer. "Is it a signed print?"

"No. It's an original."

Mack sputtered as he turned to Brantley. "Jesus. You're kidding."

"No. They're all originals." Brantley motioned through the room. "I didn't live extravagantly, so when I did spend money, it was on these."

Mack hadn't paid much attention to the art in the room, but he whistled now that he knew they weren't just for decoration. "These are... amazing."

"I like to think so."

"How did you get them here?" Mack asked.

"I had special cases made for each of them."

"Then if you're worried, I'd suggest packing them in the cases and we'll find a safe place for them until your security equipment arrives and we can get it installed." He couldn't get over having this much in art just hanging on the walls. It blew his mind. They were right out in the open. "Go on."

"Right now?"

"If you're worried about them, then take care of it now. I have a few calls to make."

Brantley set down his bag. "I put them in the bedroom." He hurried away and returned with what looked like large briefcases with handles. He set them on the floor, made a second trip, and then opened the first and transferred the painting to a white silk bag and then into the case.

Mack stepped out of the way, watching Brantley work as he talked on the phone. He had to turn away when Brantley bent down, that glorious rear end waving in the air like a red cape in front of a bull.

Brantley repeated the process with each of the other, less iconic images, the dogs watching from their perch on the sofa. "Now what do we do?"

Mack was just finishing up. "Thanks." He put his phone back in his pocket. "The truck is at the sheriff's department garage. Now we need to transfer the art to the trunk." He hoped there was room. "I called a friend at the bank. They have a secondary vault within the main one. At one time, they held gold from the Black Hills here on its way East. So they put in the extra security, and most of the time it's empty now. They'll rent it to you."

"Oh God, that would be a huge load off my mind." Brantley and Zeb took the cases out to the car, and after moving some of Zeb's equipment to the floor of the backseat, they got them into the trunk and gently closed it.

Brantley got his bag, and Mack gathered the dogs. The car was loaded to the gills with everything once they left. Zeb drove them to the bank, where Brantley and the bank manager transferred the art into the vault. Then Zeb drove them home. Brantley went inside with his bag and the dogs, and Mack got into his cruiser to go into the station for a bit. He wanted to stay and keep Brantley safe, but the best way he could do that was to find out who was behind all this, and maybe without being distracted by every move Brantley made, he could make some progress.

CHAPTER 4

BRANTLEY KEPT waiting for the next shoe to drop. He spent the next day with Lew, but was going a little stir-crazy. He wished he'd thought to bring his laptop with him, but he'd forgotten it in the hubbub of getting his art packed and tucked safely into the vault. It would give him something to do.

"Lew, what do you think about going for a ride? I need my computer, and we could go out to the ranch. It won't take long."

"Sounds good to me. These walls are closing in." Lew wheeled his chair toward the kitchen door. "What are you waiting for? I got my keys, and the car is in the garage."

"Okay." He hadn't expected Lew to be so excited.

"Mack thinks I'm helpless and need taking care of all the time." Lew pulled open the door and wheeled himself out of the house and down the ramp that ran along the garage wall.

After locking the door, Brantley hurried to keep up. It seemed he'd started a ball rolling and now it was picking up speed, and when all the dogs raced after him, jumping in as soon as Lew opened the car door, it was pandemonium.

Brantley wondered if he'd have to help Lew into the car, but he got in easily, and all Brantley had to do was fold the chair and slide it into the backseat. Then he got in the passenger side and closed the door. Lew raised the garage door with the opener and backed out, using the hand controls.

Good God, Lew drove like a bat out of hell, with a dog in each backseat window and Lulu on his lap, tongues hanging out, watching everything. "I haven't been out to the Richardson place, your ranch, in years," Lew said as he drove. "It used to be a real busy place. Clair Richardson was one of the premier horse experts in the state. Everyone used to bring their problem horses to her, and she'd work out their issues. Bart was a cattleman through and through. He inherited the ranch from his father and built it up over the years. My folks were close friends of theirs."

"What happened?"

"They got older. Clair couldn't handle the horses any longer, and Bart had a stroke a few years ago. They stayed on the ranch until they died, but by then it was just them on an empty ranch. They leased the land to Erickson for a while."

"That explains why he gave me such a hard time. I met Andy when I called the police because there were strange cattle on my land—they were his."

"He wanted to buy your place from them, but he never had the money. He isn't the best businessman, and his wife loves to spend money. I understand their house is full of stuff they don't need that she bought off the television." Lew was clearly amused.

Brantley once again breathed a sigh of relief when they pulled into the yard and everything looked the same as it had when he'd been there the previous evening. "I'll run in and get what I need and be right back."

"Help me get out, and I'll wheel around for a little while," Lew said. "I want to look at the place."

Brantley opened the door and let the dogs out. They took off with yips and happy barks. He got out Lew's chair and helped him transfer into it. "Do you need anything else?"

"Go and get your things," Lew said as he whirled around and took off toward the barn. "I'll be around."

Brantley watched him go for a few seconds and then went up to the house. The dogs raced around his legs, followed him in, and took off once they got inside. Once again they explored while Brantley went into his office, grabbed his bag, and shoved the laptop and cords inside, along with his notes.

"Come on, guys, it's time to go." He whistled for the dogs, then locked the door. He stepped off the porch as a truck pulled into the drive. Brantley instantly tensed, wondering what the hell Andy Erickson could want. He was tempted to call Mack and ask him to come to the ranch, but he wasn't sure if he'd be angry that Brantley had brought his dad out here, and besides, he needed to handle his own issues.

"You did this," Andy snarled as soon as he was out of his truck.

Brantley jumped as he slammed the door, striding over to him with fire in his eyes, causing Brantley to back up. Leo stood next to him, growling low in his throat. That sound must have given Andy pause because he halted his charge.

"You need to see what the hell you did." He pointed toward the truck.

"I've been in town with the sheriff. So whatever you think I've done, you're full of shit. Now get the hell off my land. I've had enough threats and attempts on my life to last me a lifetime. So either leave or I'll kick your ass into next week!"

Leo barked to accentuate his point, and Brantley patted his head.

"Look," Andy said, pointing once again.

Brantley followed him to the truck, peered in back, and turned away instantly, trying not to puke on his shoes. "What the hell is that?"

"It's one of my steers. It died of thirst because I don't have enough water, and what you have, you aren't using. I drove my herd off your land, and it was more than some of them could take. I have five more just like it."

"And you blame me because you acted like a dick instead of simply asking for what you needed." Brantley glared. "I don't know what the fuck is going on in that head of yours, but this is not my fault. I'm not using any of the water, and it flows through your land, so if you don't have enough, it's because you never planned and did what you needed to do before it got this dry. So don't go blaming me." Brantley turned away as Lew came wheeling toward him.

"What are you doing?" Lew called as he approached.

Andy lowered the back of the truck and Lew stopped.

"Why bring that here?"

"It's his fault," Andy said again.

"Are you totally stupid?" Lew fumed. "Now take that poor thing back to your place and bury it, for God's sake."

"But if he would help…," Andy said much more plaintively.

"Then you ask him like a civilized person. You don't intimidate or just take what isn't yours and deliver cow corpses to his doorstep. That's crazy and stupid. Now take that thing away and give it a proper burial."

Brantley was beginning to think that the people in this town were crazy.

"What am I supposed to do?" Andy asked.

"I suggest you pump water from the stream to watering stations. It won't take much to set up, and your cattle will get the water they need."

"I don't have the money to do anything. I tried drilling and came up with nothing. I spent all I have, and if I don't get water for the herd, I'm going to lose my ranch and livelihood." Andy closed the tailgate, pulled open his truck door, and turned to Brantley. "I don't expect you to understand at all. What does the life of a guy here in South Dakota mean to a man from New York?"

"It means just as much as anyone else. What I don't understand is why you think being a complete ass is going to get you what you need. If you're so hard up, then graze your cattle on my land for a month to give your pastures a rest. But you need to control them and make sure I don't come home to find them on my porch or something."

"Of course not." Andy smiled for the first time, relief welling in his eyes. "What do you want for it?"

"I don't know."

"How about some beef for his freezer when you butcher for yourself," Lew said. "It's the neighborly thing to do."

Andy nodded emphatically. "You got it. Definitely." He started the truck and turned around, then drove away as Brantley thought his legs would go out from under him.

"I would have made him squirm for a lot longer," Lew said. "You're too nice a person."

"He should have just asked instead of being a dick, but should his cattle suffer because of it? They didn't get the choice, and if they did, I'm sure they wouldn't have been raising their hooves." He put his hand in the air. "Please, please, I want to go home with an asshole."

"You do have a point, but somehow I doubt the cattle would raise their hooves. Maybe they'd poop their choice."

"In that case, someone misinterpreted shitting for going home with an asshole." Brantley smiled for the first time in days, and Lew looked like he was about to fall out of his wheelchair.

"You have to stop," Lew said, coughing because he was laughing so hard. "And we should go back."

The dogs had gone quiet and were circling their legs. A chill went up Brantley's spine, cold as full-on winter. He scanned all around, trying to figure out where it was coming from, but he had no idea. All he knew was he had a sudden and overwhelming sense that he was being watched, and it creeped him out. It wasn't like there were tons of places where someone could hide—the land was largely flat and open, but that also left Brantley feeling exposed. He pulled open the back door and the dogs jumped into the car. Once Lew was in, he got the chair in the back and hurried around to get in the passenger seat.

"Let's get out of here," Brantley said. "Just drive and get back to town."

Lulu climbed from the back onto his lap, and he held her like a shield.

"What about checking the house…?"

He turned to Lew. "Just drive." Brantley continued watching, dark places multiplying before his eyes.

Lew started the engine and once again did his race-car-driver impression.

Brantley kept an eye in back, making sure they weren't being followed. Not that it would be hard to anticipate where they were going, but he thought it was a smart thing to do. He saw no one and only relaxed once they were back at Mack's. Not that that was turning out to be a particularly safe place, if the incident with Mack's truck was any indication, but he felt safer there than he would out at his ranch alone.

Once they pulled into the garage and he'd helped Lew get inside, Brantley spent the rest of the day on his computer with the dogs curled around him. Lew took a nap in his chair at one point, and Brantley remained hunkered down until Mack got home about dinnertime. And he wasn't in a happy mood.

"You should have waited until I could have taken you out to get what you wanted," Mack growled when he found out where they'd been.

"It was fine, Mackenzie," Lew said. "I needed to get out, and he got his things. We were just fine. If Erickson hadn't come over, the whole thing would have been routinely dull. So lay off."

"Dad, someone is after him. What if it's Erickson? He wants the water on Brantley's land so bad, who knows what he'll do."

"Well, he's got it now, so if it's him, he should lay off."

Mack swirled back to him. "What's this?"

"He came over with a dead cow in the back of his truck. His cattle are dying, so I said he could graze them on my land for a month. I figured it was neighborly, and I'm hoping if he's the one behind this, now he'll back off." Brantley was of two minds about Andy Erickson. "I'm not using the land, and it's sitting empty, so I'm going to help him for a little while even if the guy is an asshole."

"It's your land."

"Yes, it is, and Andy Erickson will be over on my land, so it isn't going to be as empty or unwatched as it was before."

"What?" Mack asked his expression softening. "There's something you're not telling me."

Brantley looked toward the kitchen, and Mack nodded. He put his gun away, and when he walked away, Brantley followed. "I could have sworn while I was out there that I was being watched. The dogs felt it too. They clustered around us at one point and stayed close. They had been running around up until then, and if that's the case, it can't be Erickson, unless he can move really fast."

"Not to diminish your intuition, but many times we feel like we're being watched when we aren't. If you're feeling vulnerable or scared...."

"I know. But I figured I should tell you."

"As far as I'm concerned, Erickson isn't off the hook yet. I have talked to him about where he was for both incidents, and his alibi is sketchy at best. He's hiding something, and I'm going to find out what it is. Also, Erickson has military experience. He was in the army for four years, and he's a hunter. I don't have enough evidence to get a warrant for his guns, but he has the qualities we've been looking for."

"I bet there are others who fit that description as well."

"Yes, there are. I've been going through everyone in town to try to narrow the suspect pool, and it's taking time. Based on the person I saw, I eliminated the women who fit our profile."

"We're making a lot of suppositions. Like that all these incidents are related. What if they aren't?"

"My brake lines were cut. They didn't fail on their own. I think they were trying to tell us that they could get to you anywhere, even if you were here. I've seen this type of personality before. Only the last time, the suspect wasn't as well trained."

"Do you need to ask for help?" Brantley asked.

"It isn't like I can bring in the FBI by making a phone call. In the grand scheme of things, this is a small case in a small town. Even though for Hartwick this is a huge deal, and I need to solve this soon, but I keep spinning my wheels. There aren't enough clues to go on, and I need a little more information. But to get it, I have to wait until they act again, and that puts you and other people in danger. But I have no idea what he'll do next."

"So let's sit down and talk about it. Sometimes talking about things will jar an idea loose," Brantley suggested.

Mack pulled out a chair but stopped when his phone rang. "What is it, Julie?" Mack asked. "Oh… all right… stay inside and lock the doors. I'm on my way." Mack hung up and dashed to the front door. "Julie said she saw a stranger on her land, and he seemed to be heading across to your place." He paused to get his gun. "Where do you think you're going?"

"With you," Brantley said, hurrying right behind him.

"Brantley, you need to stay here."

He shook his head and followed Mack outside. "We're wasting time arguing." He pulled open the door to Mack's cruiser and got in. Mack got in the driver's seat and started the engine.

"The only reason I'm not kicking you out is because it would waste time." Mack peeled out of the drive and raced out of town at near takeoff speed. Brantley hung on to the "oh shit" handle as Mack broke all speed limits. By the time they reached his neighbor's ranch, Brantley wondered if he'd shat himself.

Mack jumped out as soon as the car pulled to a stop.

Julie came over to them as Brantley got out of the car, gesturing toward the barn. "He went behind it and continued that way." Julie pointed toward his land.

"Did you get a look at him?" Mack asked.

"Thirties, maybe, wearing camo of some kind. Not sure if he was a hunter or what."

The camo description sent Brantley's heart racing and ice water pooling in his veins.

"Stay here!" Mack ordered and called for reinforcements. "You hear me?" Mack asked like Brantley was a child, and Brantley agreed, his jaw tightening. "Just go inside," Mack added less angrily, and Brantley joined Julie on the porch as Mack headed off.

"I have some tea," Julie said as she motioned him inside. She locked the door and continued through the house to the kitchen, where Nathan was having a mac-and-cheese dinner. She gestured for him to sit, and he did.

"Mr. Brantley," Nathan said happily. "I can ride my bike good now. Can I show him?" He slid down off his chair.

"You need to finish your dinner, and Mr. Mack asked us to stay inside." Julie's calm was shocking, especially since Brantley was shaking like a leaf. Thank goodness the others couldn't see his legs quaking under the table.

"But, Mom," Nathan whined. "You said I could ride if I was good." He turned back to the table.

"I saw another of those vagrants, like a few weeks ago. Mack is going to see if he can find him. We need to stay inside where it's safe."

"What about the horsies and the cattle?"

"They can take care of themselves," Julie said. "Now go ahead and finish your dinner." She tapped the table, and Nathan returned to his meal, acting like each bite was a huge chore.

"Have you had vagrants out here before?" Brantley asked as Julie placed a glass of tea in front of him.

"A few times. Guys come out West to escape or be on their own, and they end up living hand to mouth. Some of them take to the land and try to live on their own. It happened more a few years ago, during the downturn. When people are desperate, they'll try just about anything to survive. One man shot one of our herd and then tried to drag it off. I think his idea was to try to carve it up, but these are big animals."

Brantley nodded.

"I think the guy thought that once he killed it, something would magically happen and it would turn itself into steaks and hamburger. Mack caught him easily, and he worked in town for a while to pay for what he'd done and then moved on."

Brantley wasn't sure if he could relax or not. He told himself that Mack knew what he was doing. Sirens sounded and got louder, and then cruisers zipped past the ranch and headed on toward his. He felt better knowing Mack would have backup, but he hated this whole thing.

"Why did you come out here?" Julie asked.

"I wanted a change in my life," Brantley answered. "I know I could have, I don't know, moved to the beach or something, but I was hoping to get closer to the land." He drank some tea and then set the glass down. "I keep wondering if I did the right thing."

Julie nodded as she moved through the small kitchen. "This can be a very hard life, sometimes with very little reward."

"I suppose," Brantley agreed, worrying more and more.

"You can work a piece of land, pour your heart and sweat into it for years, decades, and then in a few short, lean years, it can all be taken away." She stirred something on the stove. "It's one of the facts of life out here. You know, a few years ago, when they bailed out those banks and General Motors? Because they were too big to fail or some such crap?"

"Mom, bad word," Nathan scolded.

"No one comes along to help the little guy." She continued working as she spoke.

Brantley sat still, wondering if she was speaking from personal experience or in general. He didn't want to pry into her business.

"Can I play LEGOs?" Nathan asked.

"Sure, honey." Julie turned down the stove, came over to the table, and picked up her glass. "I'm sure Mack will straighten this out and get this guy."

"Me too."

Julie absently held her ice tea without drinking. "I heard what happened to you at the diner. Did someone really take a shot at you?"

"It seems so. Mack is still trying to put all the pieces together. This whole thing is really unsettling. He has me staying with him until this is resolved. I wish I knew how long that would be or what this man is up to."

"We all do," Julie said. "I used to let Nathan out to play while I was working in the barn. Now I keep him close. It makes my work harder to do, but I don't want anything to happen to him. I want things to go back to normal just as badly as you do."

"I bet it will help to have your husband home," Brantley said.

"Right now I'm doing both our jobs. But Denny set things up pretty well before he left. He's going to have some catch-up chores to do because there is only so much I can do alone."

"Do you have people who help?"

"Not right now. I used to, but things are really tight." She looked about ready to cry, and Brantley didn't know if he should comfort her or not. "Somehow I know we'll get through it."

"I was wondering, do you give riding lessons?" Brantley asked. "I've wanted to learn to ride. It's on my list of things to do."

"Yes, though I don't do a lot of classes. A lot of the kids out here know how. It's one of the things that comes with growing up in ranch country. But I'd be happy to teach you."

"I'd pay you for your time, of course," Brantley said.

A sharp knock sounded from the back, and Nathan ran through the house. "I'll get it."

"No," Julie said sharply, and Nathan skidded to a halt in his stocking feet. "Go back and play."

He stayed where he was and waited until Julie returned with Mack behind her. "Sheriff Mack!" Nathan cried and raced to him as Brantley stood nervously.

"Hey, buddy." Mack hugged him. "Have you been good for your mom?"

"Yes," Nathan answered really quickly, and Mack reached into his pocket and handed him something.

"Put that in your bank for the next time you go to town."

Nathan nodded and hurried out of the room, clutching what Mack had given him.

"We caught up with the man crossing your land. He's as you described."

"Is he the shooter?" Brantley asked.

"We're taking him back to the station, and we'll question him, but I don't think so. He said he'd been out of work for some time. He said he was on the way to your ranch because he'd heard it was bought by a man from the city, and he was hoping you needed help," Mack explained. "We'll talk to him some more. The guy is half-starved, and from the looks of him, he's been on the road for a while."

"If you're convinced it's not him, then please make sure he's fed and help him somehow." Brantley came closer to Mack.

"There aren't a lot of social services out here."

"Does he fit what we thought?" Brantley asked. "Is he a veteran?"

"I'm going to guess he is," Mack said.

"Then when you're done, I want to talk to him," Brantley said.

Mack looked at him as though he were crazy, but Brantley had his reasons. "If that's what you want," Mack said. "I need to get back to town."

Brantley knew that was his cue; it was time for him to go as well. Brantley finished his tea and thanked Julie for her hospitality. He said good-bye to Nathan as well and followed Mack out to his cruiser.

"Did you have a good visit with Julie?" Mack asked once they were inside the car.

"She's going to teach me to ride." He wondered if he should share his other impressions. They were only that and not facts—she might have hinted at some things with him that weren't common knowledge, and it wasn't his business to say anything. He thought about telling Mack, figuring Mack would keep it to himself, but decided not to unless it became part of the case.

"That's very nice of her," Mack said in a somewhat distracted way. "You know what I hate?" he asked after a few seconds. "Investigations like this always affect more people than you ever expect."

"How so?"

"People have secrets, and sometimes those are at the heart of a crime. Most of the time they aren't, but when we're investigating a crime, everyone's secrets get brought out into the open."

"I suppose," Brantley agreed. "One of the tough things about your job is to figure out how to handle those other secrets."

"Mostly I keep things that don't involve the case to myself. If they haven't broken the law, then it really isn't my concern, and no one is perfect."

They rode the rest of the way to Mack's house.

"I'll be home late tonight. I have a lot of stuff to do."

"Okay," Brantley said, reaching across to take Mack's hand. "I know you're trying to help."

"I'll be happiest when this is over and you are able to go back to your regular life."

Brantley sighed as the car idled. "If you want the truth, I don't know what the life I'll go back to will look like. Coming out here was sort of a spur-of-the-moment decision."

"Why? Was it a bad breakup?"

"You could say that. I had a partner of sorts, but not a romantic one. I couldn't do everything on my own to manage the fund I was in charge of. There's just too much work, and my partner did some things that weren't right and tried to pin it on me. I caught wind of it and stopped him before things got bad and people lost money, but he ended up in trouble with the SEC. The side effect was that my reputation went down the shithole right along with his. And in that business, your reputation is everything. No one would touch me with a ten-foot pole. It didn't matter that I had made billions of dollars—literally—for my clients." Brantley clenched the hand that wasn't in Mack's.

"Were any charges brought against you?"

"Yes. But they were dismissed because I could prove, by sheer luck and the fact that I was with a friend, and she could verify it, when the transactions were made. The asshole hacked my account and used that to make the transactions. He bragged about it once they caught him."

"So that's why you got out?"

"Yup. And most of the people I thought were my friends ran scared. They had their own reputations to worry about, and the last thing they wanted was to be tainted by association. So I found myself on the outside of a business I once dominated." Brantley shrugged and looked away. "I needed someplace completely different and a change of scenery, so I started looking out here."

"And you stepped right into the middle of something that we can't explain."

"Exactly. I still think it's about the land. That's the only thing anyone out here could want that I have. I'm not part of the town, and I don't have a history out here."

"I checked out the people you gave me, and none of them are in the area as far as we can tell. So I'm thinking you're probably right.

But why? For the water? It isn't like you're using any of it, so the stream that flows out of it is stronger than normal and keeping the ranches downstream alive."

"Have you checked to see who else was interested in purchasing the ranch before I bought it? Maybe the realty office has records of anyone Renae showed it to."

"I checked her appointment book, and there were a few people, mostly locals, and I've eliminated them. That's what has me baffled. The usual things aren't yielding any results."

"Then we need to try something different. When I'm trying to dig out a fact about a company, I'll make some assumptions and see if their behavior fits. It sometimes yields results. So let's assume someone wants the ranch for the water—who would want it most? We don't have to worry about alibis or anything. Just make a list of potential buyers, and then we can eliminate them."

Brantley turned from staring at the garage door toward Mack and found him looking back just as intently. He was damn tempted to lean in and take those full lips. Brantley was hard just thinking about it. He wanted Mack so badly. His hands grew warm just from his touch, and heat radiated up his arm to his chest before spreading through the rest of him. Was it lust or something more? At the moment, he wasn't sure, and it didn't matter much.

"I'll see what I can dig up, and we'll talk it over when I get home. Have you been approached directly by anyone?" Mack asked.

"Not that I would sell, but no. I don't want to let it go. It's a great piece of land."

"How do you know that?"

"Because I think someone wants it pretty badly, and if that's true, then it must have some real value. In my former business, you learn that something is only of worth or valuable when someone else wants it badly. It seems someone might want my ranch badly enough to kill for it. Renae sold me the ranch, and they killed her and took a shot at me. They also cut your brake lines. I think most of this is a fear campaign. If I leave town and put the ranch up for sale, they're betting I'll sell it cheap just to get rid of it."

"Okay," Mack said. "But we're no closer to who that could be." He sighed softly. "Let me get together a list of people who might have been interested and go through Renae's appointment book again for any more clues. We can review it tonight when I get home."

Brantley let go of Mack's hand and got out of the car. He went right inside, while Mack drove off to work.

"How did it go with Julie? Was it him?" Lew asked.

"Mack doesn't think so. This whole thing is frustrating."

"Give it time. People make mistakes, and this guy is going to make one too."

"Hopefully before I'm dead, though," Brantley groused and then wished he hadn't. Mack was doing his best, and this situation wasn't his fault. It was the fault of the son of a bitch who'd killed Renae. Brantley hoped to hell he got the chance to look the asshole in the eye and take a swing at him. "Have you eaten? Do you want me to help make something?"

"I was waiting for you and Mack to get back." Lew wheeled himself into the kitchen, and Brantley followed. Most things had been brought down to Lew's level. "I made some chili, so all we need to do is heat it up."

"Thanks, Lew," Brantley said. "I know this whole thing is an inconvenience, and I'm sorry. I hope to get out of your hair as soon as I can."

"Like you're an inconvenience. Most of the time I sit here all day pretty much alone except for the pack, and they don't talk much. You ain't a burden or nothing." Lew got two plates and bowls, then set them on the table. "Have you heard about your truck?"

"They said it's going to take another week. There are lots of parts they have to order, apparently." He had thought of just buying another new truck and saying to hell with it, but spending money just to spend it was a waste in Brantley's book. He was a lot of things, but never wasteful if he could help it.

"You can use my car if you need to. You can drive it regular and not use the hand controls," Lew said as he put the first bowl in the microwave.

"I appreciate the offer." He hoped his truck would be done soon, but it warmed him that Lew had offered his vehicle. Most of his friends in New York wouldn't have done that.

"Have you met many people in town?"

"Well, let's see. You know I met Erickson, and he was pretty much a jerk."

"Yeah, but I bet that changes in a hurry. You're saving his ass, and he better remember that."

"I met my neighbor Julie and her son, Nathan. They're good people, and she's going to teach me to ride. I haven't met the people on the other side of me."

"To the north, that would be Cal and Martha Younger," Lew said.

"Cal...," Brantley said, trying to remember where he'd heard that name. "Huge guy, face that looks like he's been in one too many fights?"

"Oh, you have met him. That man was shot at and missed, crapped at and hit, but he's a dang good rancher."

Brantley swallowed. "He was at the diner when Mack took me." He didn't think it was necessary to go into their little altercation. "I'm hoping that once people realize I didn't kill anyone, they'll come around. I suppose being shot at through the diner window isn't making me hugely popular either."

"Folks will understand. It just takes some time. It would have even without this whole nasty business. People around here are good, and they look out for their neighbors. We don't get many strangers, though, and it will take some time for them to warm to you. You're a nice guy, and they'll figure that out once they get to know you." The microwave beeped, and Lew carefully took out the steaming bowl of chili and set it on the counter. He put the second one in and started heating it. "I have coffee, but if you want something else, help yourself."

When the second bowl was hot, Brantley brought crackers to the table, along with napkins. Then he set the bowls on the table and waited for Lew to take his place. "This looks really good."

"Everyone does chili different. In Wisconsin, they add macaroni. I don't like that. And Texans will tell you that chili doesn't have beans in it, but I like them."

"Me too." Brantley took a single bite, and the flavor exploded in his mouth. Lew's chili was spicy, with plenty of onions, heat, and lots of meat. He ate a lot of crackers and drank tons of water.

Once they'd finished their bowls, Lew pulled a bowl of fruit from the refrigerator, and they both scarfed down the cool fruit to put out the mouth fires.

"That chili is something else."

"Too spicy?" Lew asked.

"Nope. Just cumulative." Brantley grinned and felt like he'd passed some sort of test. They finished their coffee, and then Brantley took care of the dishes. As he stood at the lowered sink, his hands in dishwater, he stared out the window as the wind blew through the trees, and he pondered how long it had been since he'd been part of a family, like this. Well, this wasn't his family, but being here temporarily was nice.

"Where are your people? Your family?" Lew asked from the other room.

"They're a real mess." Brantley was glad he was in the other room so he wouldn't have to see Lew's expression. "My dad is a teacher at a college of divinity in Virginia. He helps turn out crops of fire and brimstone. My mom is a devoted wife, which means she goes along with whatever my father says and acts like one of those bobblehead dolls you see in cars. They raised me and my two sisters the best they knew how, but they weren't prepared when I told them I was gay." He held his breath. He wasn't sure if Lew knew about Mack or not.

"Big deal," Lew said. "Mack told me about himself when he was eighteen. He's my son and I'm proud of him no matter what he does."

Brantley took that as Lew accepting him as well. "My family and I agreed in a dish-throwing, yelling, and 'you're going to hell' sort of way that it would be best if I didn't stay around any longer. So

70

I went off to college and pretty much left them behind. I always knew that being gay was something my father could never understand or accept." He rinsed the bowls and put them in the dish drainer.

"Then he wasn't a real father," Lew said as he wheeled himself into the kitchen. "Parents are supposed to accept and support their children. Being gay is part of who you are, and you can't change it, so rejecting you for something as stupid as that is just dumb."

"It went against my father's core beliefs, and rather than change them, he rejected me. I accepted it a long time ago. I hear from my younger sister every once in a while. She's a junior in college, and she's really starting to think for herself and get out of Dad's shadow. My mother never will, and my older sister is just like her." Brantley rinsed the silverware and glasses before letting out the water, then cleaned the sink and wiped his hands.

"Any man would be proud to have a son like you." Lew patted his arm twice and then left the kitchen again, rendering Brantley dumbfounded. People seldom surprised him, but Lew had just accepted without batting an eyelash what his entire family had rejected.

"You know I knew about you already," Lew said from the other room. "I've seen the way you look at Mack."

Brantley swallowed hard. "I think a lot of him. It takes a strong man to admit when he's wrong, and Mack not only did that but has gone beyond what anyone else would do to try to keep me safe."

Lew came back into the kitchen. "You know that the way you look at Mack is the same way he looks at you. Mack has been alone for quite a while, and it's a shame. He has a lot to offer, and I want him to be happy." Lew went back into the living room, and when Brantley joined him, he was shifting to his chair. "It's been just him and me for so many years."

"Mack said his mother left when he was young," Brantley said, and Lew nodded, settling into his chair with a sigh.

"His mother was gorgeous. Her name was Liliana, and I called her Lily because she reminded me of a simple, beautiful flower. I wooed her, and after we married, we moved to be closer to my family. We could have lived on the reservation, but I could get work here and there were no jobs on the reservation. I think that was my first mistake. Taking Lily away from her people and the life she knew was too much. But Lily didn't complain. She and I were happy and in love. After two years, she got pregnant, and then we had the excitement of the birth to look forward to and everything was good. But after Mack was born, Lily went through bouts of deep depression. She'd go to bed for days and needed help I couldn't give her."

"Postpartum depression can be a terrible thing," Brantley said.

"I think it was for Lily. She took care of Mack and was a good mother, but she was lonely, and eventually she came to me and said that she wanted to go home. I asked if she needed someone to talk to. I made an appointment with a doctor, but she didn't go to the appointment and left Mack with a neighbor before going back to the reservation."

"Did she see Mack after that?"

"No. I got a call from her brother a few weeks later that Lily had taken her own life." Lew wiped his eyes on his sleeve. "So it's been Mack and me ever since. I raised him and tried to be both mom and dad to him. It wasn't easy."

"Do you ever talk about her with Mack?"

"No. He doesn't remember her. He knows what happened, and I've tried to keep him focused forward, rather than on the past. I have a few pictures of Lily around, but I never framed them and put them up. There was no need. I always answered Mack's questions honestly, but she was gone, and we had lives to lead. Lily wasn't coming back."

It was clear that Lew still missed his wife. "This is still hard for you, isn't it?"

"You wouldn't think so after all these years, but it is. Friends encouraged me to date again, and I did a few times, but it didn't feel right. And I had a hard time trusting again, so nothing ever happened." Lew put the recliner up. "Sometimes when I'm asleep, I see her in my dreams." Lew smiled and turned on the television, signaling that the heart-baring and soul-rending portion of the evening was at an end.

Brantley got his computer and sat with it on his lap while Lew watched TV and dozed in his chair. As the evening wore on, Lew said good night and went to bed. Brantley whiled away the time, waiting for Mack, who finally arrived home at nearly ten.

"Is Dad asleep?" Mack asked softly when he came through the door.

"Yeah," Brantley said as he looked up from the screen, the dogs all curled around him. They jumped down and circled Mack for pats and scratches. Then Lulu walked down the hall, most likely to Lew's room, and the others settled back on the sofa.

"What a night. The guys and I went over everything, and we're no further ahead. I have them trying to run down a few things, but our leads are petering out fast." He put his gun away and took off his belt and hat, then loosened his shirt buttons. "I know we were going to go over some things, but I'm so tired, I can barely think straight." Mack flopped onto the sofa next to Brantley.

"I've been working on a few things," Brantley said. "There's Andy Erickson, who wants my land for the water. But you said he has an alibi." And he'd hate to think that he was actually helping the guy who'd caused all this trouble. That would be a load of shit. "You said it was a man you saw outside the house the other night, so that rules Julie out."

Mack nodded. "True. Julie doesn't have military training, but she is a hunter. Erickson has military training as well. His alibi is a little weak, but he has one. I can press him for more if it comes to it, but he says he was with his wife, and she doesn't deny it. I need to look into him further. There was something that bothered me."

"And I found out that the Neanderthal at the diner is my other neighbor. Have you looked into Cal Younger to see if he has an alibi?"

"I did and he doesn't. Cal said he was at home when Renae was killed, and he was in the diner when the window was shot, so either the incidents aren't connected or Cal is off the list."

"So that takes care of my neighbors and most of the people I've met since I got here."

"The Clark place runs across the street from you, but they have water and are big enough that if they wanted the land, they could afford to buy it outright, so I doubt it's them."

"Then there has to be someone else, or we're missing an important detail." Brantley closed the lid to his laptop. "I don't know the people here well enough to be asking a bunch of questions."

"I'm going to pay visits to everyone tomorrow. It's time to shake the tree and see if anything falls out." Mack yawned and stood with a groan. Then he left the room, half dragging his feet down the hall.

Brantley watched him go, disappointment blooming inside and spreading like spilled tar. For most of the day, he'd looked forward to Mack coming home. Just seeing Mack was enough to get his heart beating faster. Maybe he didn't have the same effect on Mack. Brantley turned off the television—he'd been ignoring it anyway—and put out the lights before going to the guest room. He sat on the side of the bed, listening as the water ran in the bathroom.

He wasn't going to blame Mack if he was too tired or had forgotten about their make-out session the night before. Brantley had to remember that just because he'd felt something, or thought he had, didn't mean Mack had felt the same thing. He'd made that mistake more than once in the past. Johnny came to mind first thing. Brantley thought they'd had a connection, but all Johnny had wanted was to try to cash in on him. Brantley didn't think that was what Mack wanted, but he had been wrong before, and all the insecurity he'd endured after Johnny dumped him threatened to push its way forward. Maybe he just wasn't meant to have a boyfriend.

Brantley was so deep in his own head, he hadn't noticed the water stop or the bathroom door open. But he couldn't help noticing the wide shoulders and light copper skin as Mack stood in his doorway.

"I feel so much better," Mack whispered and took a step into the room. "Did you think I'd forgotten you?"

Brantley refused to acknowledge what he'd feared.

Leo raced by Mack, jumped onto the bed, and settled at the bottom, with Rex not far behind.

"Guys, get off," Mack said, and they jumped down, looking like they'd been denied food for a week. "Go sleep in the living room." Once they'd left, Mack closed the door. His gaze turned to Brantley, simmering. He stalked closer, towel swinging slightly, a bulge in the most important place.

Brantley lifted his gaze, raking it over Mack's narrow waist and up his tight belly, which rippled slightly with each breath. He reached out, running his finger over a pink line above Mack's hip.

"That's where I was shot the first time. The bullet grazed me, but it hurt like hell."

"And this?" Brantley asked, running his hand up Mack's side to a long scar on his shoulder. "Another bullet?"

"Yeah. It goes with the job and the life." Mack stilled. "A lot of people can't handle it."

Brantley nodded. The depth of the pain in Mack's voice spoke of personal experience. "I can handle just about anything," Brantley said. The scars brought into clear relief how dangerous Mack's job could be, but it seemed that, out here, anyone could be in danger, and it was Mack's job to keep everyone safe. Brantley leaned closer, bringing his lips in contact with Mack's belly, kissing along one of the ripples.

Mack cupped Brantley's cheeks in his large, hot hands, tilting his head upward until their gazes locked together with laser intensity. "I know you can." He leaned down and brought their lips together.

The room grew very warm as Mack intensified the kiss, pushing him back onto the soft mattress. It cradled him as Mack added more of his weight. He smelled of soap and shampoo mixed with musk and desire. Brantley held Mack tightly, running his hands down his powerful back until he reached the edge of the towel. He yanked, and the terrycloth came away in his hand. Brantley dropped it to the floor and smoothed his hands over Mack's firm butt. "I want you, Mack."

"And I want you." Mack sucked on Brantley's ear. "I'm going to get you naked so I can finally look at you in all your enticing glory. Then I'm going to make you pant and shake for me."

"I have little doubt of that." Brantley was damn near shaking as it was, and while Mack was naked, he was still fully clothed. Though he got the idea that he wasn't going to be for very much longer.

"Let's get this shirt off," Mack growled, pulling at the hem and tugging it over his head and off his arms.

Damn, it felt right and amazing when Mack's chest met his. Skin to skin. He wanted to writhe just so he could rub against him. Hell, Brantley did it anyway until Mack stilled him and pulled open his belt and pants, then yanked them off his legs.

Mack stood next to the bed, staring intently at him. Brantley squirmed again, hoping Mack liked what he saw. Mack scooped him up and placed him with his head on the pillows.

"I feel like a teenager," Brantley said.

"Why?"

"I swear I'm going to come just watching you."

Mack climbed back onto the bed, and Brantley used the proximity to close his fingers around Mack's cock—thick, hot, and long. He stroked, and Mack quivered above him. Damn, that was heady—a strong man like Mack shaking for him.

"You need to give me a chance to breathe, because thinking unsexy thoughts certainly isn't working. You've pushed everything else from my head except you," Mack said, and took his mouth in a kiss that drove everything from Brantley's head. Shootings, truck brakes, fears, worry—they all shot out of him like they never existed, and Brantley clung to Mack. He slid his legs along Mack's rough ones, their chests filling with air and pressing together. Brantley pushed Mack's hips to his, thrusting upward just to get a hint of friction.

"Sweetheart," Mack breathed into his ear. "Just take your time. We have all night."

"Do we? What if someone comes and tries to sabotage your truck again, or shoots through the window?"

"Then we'll stop. But it's going to take something like that to get me to walk away from you right now." Mack traced his finger along Brantley's jaw. "Just let that go." He slid his finger down Brantley's neck and throat, and Brantley stretched to give him better access. Mack leaned forward and licked under his jaw and along his neck.

"Damn," Brantley breathed and gripped the bedding in tight fists as Mack sucked his chest, clamping a nipple between his greedy lips. Brantley thrust his chest forward, desperately wanting more. He needed everything, wanted it all at once. He wasn't sure where to put his hands and ended up lying back on the bed while Mack had his way with him. "God!" Brantley groaned. He was afraid he was too loud, but Mack didn't wait any longer, sliding his lips down Brantley's shaft, encasing him in scorching wetness that sent lightning surging through his veins.

"That's it, sweetheart," Mack said when he came up for air. "You taste like sweet honey." Mack flashed him a smile and then sucked him into his mouth once again.

Brantley had been staring cross-eyed at the ceiling, but he raised his head—he had to see his cock sliding between Mack's lips. God, that had to be the hottest sight he'd seen in a long time, and the way Mack smoothed his hands over Brantley's belly and hummed around his cock sent little jolts of desire through him and was nearly enough to send Brantley over the edge.

"I can't last...," he pleaded, desperately wanting to hold him and last a little longer.

Mack thankfully backed away, and Brantley flopped back on the bed.

"You...," he moaned as he gasped for air. "Were the one... who said... we had... all night."

"We definitely do, but I wanted to give you a sample, and I couldn't resist a taste of you." Mack sat back and rolled Brantley onto his belly. Then Mack stretched out on top of him, his cock pressing along Brantley's ass.

Brantley pushed back against him, moaning when Mack sucked at the back of his neck and then slid down his back. He yipped when Mack lightly bit one of his buttcheeks. "What are you doing?" he asked with a smile, nearly ready to chuckle. The sound died in his throat when Mack pressed apart his asscheeks and buried his face between them, licking his opening, sending Brantley into orbit. "Man...."

"Has no one ever rimmed you before?" Mack asked, then blew on his wet skin, threatening to blow the top off Brantley's head.

"No." He whimpered like a baby, wanting more but afraid to ask for it. Mack seemed to understand and sucked at his cheeks. Brantley had never considered himself a butt man. He'd liked anal sex and all, though he'd never been over the moon for it, but whatever Mack was doing to him had him wondering just what he'd been missing out on all these years.

"I know I can be a little pushy and demanding, so if I do something you don't like, just say so," Mack said.

"I... ah... I...." Brantley gave up. The only thing he didn't like was the fact that he was looking at the pillowcase instead of Mack's studliness.

Mack slipped away, and Brantley wound his arms under the pillow, stretching out, wondering what glorious sensation was next. "You look so ready for me," Mack whispered as his warmth surrounded him, hovering right above him.

"I am, but is that fair?" Brantley slowly rolled over.

Mack held himself above him on his thick arms and then lowered himself down, covering Brantley and sending fire radiating through him. "Honey, it's more than fair." He stroked Brantley's cheek. "Do you have any idea what you do to me?"

"Me?" Brantley clutched Mack in case he changed his mind and pulled away. "I'm not the one all full of huge muscles. I'm skinny and nerdy. I've spent my life indoors, so I'm pale and pasty." Brantley shimmied away and sat up. "You're the one all tan and warm, with eyes as deep as the night and hair that makes me want to run my fingers through it as I wonder what it would feel like to have these silky strands wrapped around my cock." Brantley put his hand over his mouth as he realized he'd actually said those words out loud. A wicked little fantasy was one thing, but to actually say it out loud was something else. He blushed like a teenager and turned away from Mack.

"Is that what you really want?" Mack asked. "You have a thing about my hair?"

"Yeah, I do. But I didn't mean to say that. It's totally embarrassing. Just forget it, okay?" He wanted to crawl under the bed and hide forever. Hell, maybe the floor would swallow him up.

"Sweetheart, we all have our fantasies. Right now I'm thinking about what it would be like to slide inside you so deep, you feel me for days," Mack whispered just loud enough for Brantley to hear. It sent a shiver through him, and his eyes lost focus for a few seconds.

"God, Mack."

"Is that okay?" Mack parted his legs and settled between.

"I can't believe you want me," Brantley breathed.

"I don't know the source of that insecurity, but I intend to do my best to wipe it from your memory." Mack leaned closer. "See, you have this adorable little line that goes from your hip…." Mack traced it with the tip of his finger, and Brantley wasn't sure if he was going to giggle or groan.

"I'm a nerdy guy who spends his days behind a computer."

"You're adorable."

Brantley would never have admitted to anyone that being described as adorable or cute was a turn-on, but coming from Mack, it definitely was. He'd take being adorable if feeling alive and like the center of the universe came with it. Mack certainly made him feel that way.

"Did you ever see yourself with a county sheriff?" Mack said.

"I haven't seen myself with anyone for a very long time," Brantley admitted, and he wondered if he was going to have to adjust his image of himself. It was too soon to really put the two of them together in his head. Things didn't usually work out for him in the romance department, and he was scared.

"I understand that." Mack made little circles with his finger around Brantley's belly button.

Brantley held his breath as Mack slowly rose from the bed and reached over to the nightstand. He pulled open the drawer and took out a bottle and packet before jamming it closed again. "Do you always keep condoms in here?"

"No. I suppose it was a 'hope springs eternal' sort of thing." Mack returned his attention to him, quickly using his lips to make Brantley forget all about it. "I want you, sweetheart. I want to be inside you, with you. If it's too soon, please tell me."

"Too soon?" Brantley asked, tugging Mack down into a kiss. It was his turn to take Mack's lips. It hadn't occurred to him that Mack might have been hurt the same way he was or that there could be an ounce of insecurity in him. "No. It's not."

"I've been told I'm too aggressive—" Mack began, but Brantley cut him off with a demanding kiss.

Now was not the time for explanations. Brantley understood aggression. He hadn't become the manager of a hedge fund by sitting back and letting it happen. He knew aggression because he had it as well, just focused in a different way. For him, physical aggression—contained and not meant to hurt, but to please—was the sexiest concept he could get his head around. So when Mack prepared himself and then got into position, pressing into him with banked power, Brantley met his steely gaze with one of his own.

"Fuck…," Mack groaned, and Brantley arched his back when Mack breached him and then slowly slid deeper. The stretch and burn were overwhelming but settled quickly. What drove Brantley's eyes to cross and made his skin tingle was the warm feeling of completeness that descended over him. It didn't last long, because the heat Mack poured out was too great to ignore, but he loved that contentment for as long as it lasted.

"Damn," Brantley moaned when Mack stilled, as if he were afraid to move. When Mack did finally move, he groaned. They moved together slowly, deliberately. Like Mack had said earlier, they had all night, and he seemed intent on taking his time, building the desire and passion slowly, stoking the fire one piece at a time until it turned into a raging inferno that Brantley feared might consume him completely.

Time stood still. Hours and minutes outside their bubble meant nothing as Brantley held Mack tight, urging him forward, wanting all he was willing to give—until he could hold back no more and cried out his release into Mack's shoulder as Mack followed right behind him.

Brantley gasped and lay back, closing his eyes, letting the experience settle over him. Mack slowly pulled away and took care of what he needed to, then joined Brantley on the bed, tugging him close. They were alone, behind a closed door, and for a few seconds, Brantley could imagine that they were safe and that the world couldn't touch them, but that was, of course, an illusion. The danger stalking him would show up once again, and they needed to be ready.

CHAPTER 5

LATE THE following morning, Mack drove out to pay a visit to a few folks. There was too much he didn't know, and he was determined to get some answers. As he drove, he hummed to himself, something he hadn't done in a long time. Happiness was a great thing, but he knew it could be fleeting, even more so if he didn't get to the bottom of whatever the hell was happening. His humming died away when he reached the drive he was looking for and pulled in.

"Cal," Mack called once he was parked and got out of the cruiser.

"What are you doing out here? I didn't do nothing," Cal said quickly as he limped toward him.

"Are you sure?"

"Is this about what happened at Maggie's Roadhouse? Van Der Veen started it. I was only defending myself." Cal put his hands on his hips in order to puff himself up and seem threatening. It didn't work.

"No one said anything to us, so whatever happened must have been worked out." Mack stepped closer. "When are you going to grow up?" He looked around. Maybe Cal was spending too much time at the bars and not enough at home taking care of business.

"I'm fine," he argued.

"This place isn't and you know it. What the hell happened?"

"Martha left and went to her sister's." Cal deflated like a balloon. "The worst part is that I didn't do what she thinks I did." He sounded more like a wounded little boy than a man who threw hundred-pound sacks of feed around like they were nothing.

"What does she think you did?" Mack asked.

"Someone told her I was having an affair with that real estate agent who was killed. I never cheated on Martha, and I know who said something too. Erickson is trying to push the pile of shit off his doorstep and onto mine."

"Andy Erickson was seeing Renae Montgomery?" Mack asked, his mind turning fast. That changed everything and would give Erickson a definite motive for murder.

"Yeah. I saw them together two weeks ago. They were riding out of town in his truck. I pulled to a stop next to them and saw her trying to hide. But I knew it was her, and Erickson looked like he'd been caught with his hand in the cookie jar. Marlene at the diner saw them together too, and she said they were too close and too giggly to have been there just as friends. Then Erickson told Martha that Renae and I were seeing each other, and Martha took off to her sister's."

"And you went to the Roadhouse, drank too much, and got into a fight?" Mack shook his head and got back to why he came. "I want to talk to you about where you were last Monday afternoon."

"When that troublemaking bitch was killed? I was here working. So was Art Wenzel. He delivered cattle feed." Cal became animated. "Wait, I can prove it." He pulled open the door to his truck and fished through some papers on the passenger seat. "Art always puts the time of delivery on his receipts because he says he needs it for his records. I don't know why, but.... Here it is!" Cal returned, pressed the paper into Mack's hand, and pointed to the time in Art's chicken scratches. "We finished unloading the truck at four, and it took over an hour. Art stayed for some ice tea after we were done. I offered him a beer, but he said he was driving. You can check with him, but I was here working and I didn't shoot her. Why would I?"

Mack put the receipt in a plastic bag and labeled it. "I'll give this back when I'm done." The receipt put Cal here on his ranch during the most likely time of Renae's murder and well after. Not that he suspected that Cal had actually done it, but it was good to officially eliminate him, and he now had another great lead. "Cal, call Martha and tell her what happened."

"She won't talk to me."

"Then make her listen. I suggest you clean this place up, get some flowers, and then go over and see her. If you love Martha, then show her."

"But what if she doesn't believe me?"

"Cal, did Renae ever make a pass at you?"

He shook his head. "She never even spoke to me other than to ask who someone else was."

"Then maybe there's something else behind this other than Renae. Talk to Martha and find out. Maybe she isn't happy, and if that's the case, you need to know so you can fix it. Maybe think about her more than you do about going out to the Roadhouse all the time." Mack patted Cal on the shoulder. "She deserves a full-time husband who cares for her more than he does a beer or his buddies." Mack got back into his car. He pulled out and saw Cal getting to work. He really hoped Cal did something because there was no way on earth he would ever find someone else as good as Martha.

Mack left the ranch and did another pass in front of Brantley's, pulling in to make sure everything was okay and then going the country miles around to the Erickson ranch.

"Mack," Erickson said as he came out of the house.

"This isn't a social call," Mack said tersely. "I need to talk to you."

"I'm busy at the moment."

"Then we'll do this the hard way and I'll take you into the station for questioning." Mack was tired of playing around. "You lied to me, and I intend to get to the bottom of this." He unlatched his gun, ready to go for it at any second.

Erickson nodded and walked over toward the nearest paddock, and Mack followed, keeping a safe distance between them.

"Why didn't you tell me about you and Renae? Was it a one-time thing or had the two of you been carrying on for a while?"

"I met the bitch at the Watering Hole one night when I'd had too much to drink, and I ended up fucking her. It was stupid, and she tried to blackmail me with it. I told her to go ahead, I was going to tell Grace about it anyway, but then I find out that she's dead. I was so relieved, and I figured she'd done to someone else what she tried to do to me and it got her killed."

"Where were you Monday afternoon?"

"Like I told you before, I was here working, trying to get water to the cattle so they didn't fucking die on me. Grace was home, and she knows where I was and that my truck didn't leave."

"It would have been a hike, but you could have walked over and killed her."

"Fine. If you don't believe me, then you can check out my guns. I have nothing to hide. She wasn't worth this much trouble," Erickson said, and Mack wanted to smack him.

"She was a person just like anyone else, and she may have liked her fun, but she didn't deserve to die for it any more than you do. Maybe we should ask Grace and get her opinion?" These people's secrets were a bunch of crap—too many secrets.

"No. I'll get the guns." Erickson went inside, and Mack tensed, ready at a second's notice to take him out. Andy came out carrying a rifle and a shotgun, both in cases. He handed them to Mack, who looked inside and checked them out.

"This is it?"

"Yeah, Grace hates the things and only lets me keep the two for hunting. And they have to be locked up. She's scared to death our boy will get into them. You know about what happened to her brother?"

"That was a shame." Mack understood. Grace's brother had killed himself when he was eight years old, playing with one of their daddy's guns. It had been the ultimate gun-safety lesson for the entire county. "He was in my class." Mack handed the shotgun back to Andy. It was the wrong type and caliber. The other one he put in his trunk. "I'll check this out, and it better not match. And if you decide to take any trips, I will come after you." The evidence he had was circumstantial, but it was mounting.

"I didn't kill her or anyone," Andy said again forcefully. "I know I have a temper, but I don't go around shooting people."

"Let's hope not," Mack retorted, wanting to keep Andy a little unbalanced. "I'll be in touch." He got back in his car and pulled out of the drive, heading back toward town. He would need to test fire this gun and see if the bullets were close to the ones they'd recovered. It wasn't as exact as if he had his own crime lab, but if he did it himself, it wouldn't take weeks either.

Somehow he felt like he was getting closer. Even if Andy proved innocent, he had eliminated one more suspect and could move on. This was the thing about police work that he liked to think he was best at—he was dogged. He took things one step at a time and didn't look for the easy answer or expect things to simply fall into his lap. Solving cases required determination, and that was something he had plenty of.

On his way in, he pulled into the drive at home and hurried inside. His dad was in his usual spot, in front of the television, napping, and Brantley sat on the sofa with his computer on his lap.

"Someone's smiling. Does that mean you found something?" Brantley asked.

Mack leaned closer, inhaling deeply just to get a good whiff of Brantley's earthy scent. After last night, it was hard for him to concentrate. His mind kept traveling back to Brantley and his intense eyes and warm smile. Not to mention the other parts of him that he had to push from his mind for fear of complete embarrassment. "I did. At least I hope so. This case is turning out to have more twists than I expected." He sat down next to Brantley. "Andy had a fling with Renae. That's what he was holding back. He says he didn't kill her and that his wife can verify at least part of his story."

"Does she know?"

"Andy says no, and it's up to him to tell her. I tend to believe him, but I'm checking further into it as well."

"What about my other neighbor?"

"It seems Andy tried to throw him under the bus, and I have to check his alibi, but I don't think he did it either."

"So we're back where we started."

"Maybe. If Renae had a fling with Andy, I wonder who else she did the horizontal hula with. I'm going to check her appointment book." Mack paused. There was something else he wanted to tell Brantley. "William Turner, the vagrant we picked up crossing your land, turned out to just be a man down on his luck. We got him in touch with one of the local churches, and they're taking him under their wing to try to get him back on his feet."

That got a smile. "Good." Brantley looked at his screen and then back at him. "Do you want some help?" he asked, setting his computer aside. "I'm getting so tired of sitting here all the time. Not that Lew isn't good company."

His dad snored even louder, as if to prove Brantley's point. "Okay. You're the one who says he likes puzzles, so maybe you can make heads or tails of her appointment book. She seemed to have a code that she used for some of the entries."

"Okay." Brantley closed his computer and put it back in his bag. He gathered the cord as well. "Tell your dad where we're going, and then let's go." He was already heading for the door.

Mack chuckled to himself. Brantley must have been bored. Mack hated to wake his dad, but did anyway and explained where they were going. His dad nodded and shooed them along. He was half back to snoring again when Mack locked the door and they headed to the station.

The station was quiet since the deputies on duty were out patrolling. The building had been built some fifty years before, and it looked it. Most of the desks were old sixties gray metal, but they were serviceable and the budget didn't allow for replacements. Mack liked to joke that if they kept them much longer, they'd be antiques and he could sell them to pay for the replacements. "Have a seat, and I'll get the appointment book."

Mack went into the evidence locker and pulled out the red leather-covered book and returned to the desk. Brantley had already set up his computer, and Mack helped him log on to the Internet. "Okay. Some of the entries are pretty clear, with names, addresses, and times. I expect those are showings, and I was able to match them with recent sales. But there are these others that are just initials. I thought they were the men she was with, but I'm not so sure now."

Brantley took a look and worked his way through some of the pages. "Maybe the names of the men didn't matter," he suggested. "If Renae was out for a good time, maybe the guys were notches on her bedpost. So maybe these are certain characteristics that she liked." He began running through the book. "Did you ever find her phone?"

"No. But I got records. She did a lot of texting, but I don't have the messages."

"Hmmm." Brantley went through the book page by page. "This could be something that only meant anything to her, and if that's the case, we may never figure it out. But there is a pattern. See, there are only these entries on Saturdays and Wednesdays. Did she only go out those nights?"

"I hadn't noticed that," Mack said. He wondered if once he cleared Andy, he could ask him exactly when they had their tryst. He should have gotten that information when he talked to him.

"I think some of these are her version of texting abbreviations. She never expected anyone else to see this."

"So, what, these are conquest entries?" Mack asked.

"Why not? From what I've heard, Renae was a cougar, and she was up for a little sexual adventure. She was attractive and seemed like a strong, independent woman. If she wanted male companionship, why shouldn't she have it? If the roles were reversed, we'd say the guy was a stud."

"So what does T.I.B. mean?"

"It could be something as simple as Tiger in Bed. I don't know." Brantley continued to look through the book. "Here's one: D.F. I like Dead Fish for that one." He chuckled. "Unfortunately I don't really know. They aren't texting abbreviations in common use. So they're something she made up. It isn't like she put a codex in here."

"Why is it that nothing in this case makes sense? The three people to whom your land would be most valuable don't seem to be the ones who are trying to scare you off," Mack observed. "And the victim is telling us very little. I wish we had her phone. There could be something of value on it."

"Unless it was locked, and then we'd have to break into it."

Mack rolled his eyes.

"Okay." Brantley put the planner aside. "This is getting us nowhere. We made an assumption that I was being scared away because of the water on my land. But what if that isn't true? What if there's something else?"

"Like what?"

"I don't know," Brantley said.

Mack groaned. "I'm going to verify these last alibis and check on this gun. I also need to call Andy's wife to confirm the number of guns he has." He stood and walked to his office. The whole thing was making his head hurt.

"Do you have a land plot map of the area?"

"Sure," Mack said. "Gloria can get it for you. She's able to get her hands on anything and everything."

"Thanks." Brantley headed over toward where she sat at Dispatch, and Mack went to work making calls. He got in touch with Grace Erickson, and she confirmed that her husband only had two guns.

"What's this about, Mack?"

"Just not leaving a stone unturned." He tried to reassure her and then hung up. He was able to confirm Cal's feed delivery, and that pretty much left him out. The list of suspects kept shrinking, and Mack wasn't sure where to go from there. Renae's planner had yielded nothing at all and remained just as mysterious as it had when he'd initially found it. Mack hung up from his last call and stared at his wall of notes, hoping like hell that something would jump out at him.

"Mack," Brantley said after knocking on his doorframe. "Can you take a look at something for me?"

"Sure." He wasn't getting anywhere fast.

Brantley put the plot map on his desk. "Look at this. The spring originates here, right at the western edge of my property, and then flows east. It's quite robust, and I suspect that in the springtime there's quite a torrent flowing down it."

"Yeah, there is. Sometimes it floods when there's a large snowpack and it melts quickly. That run handles drainage for all the land downstream. Why?"

"Look at the curves. It flows here and makes a sweeping bend before it leaves my land and crosses onto Erickson's for a brief stint. Then it pretty much flows straight for a long way, at least to the end of this plot map."

"All right. I'm not sure what you're getting at."

"I don't know for sure. But what if they aren't after the water itself, but what's in the water?" Brantley bounced from foot to foot. "What if the stream has laid something bare or brought up something from deeper in the earth that someone wants."

Mack leaned closer. "You mean, like, gold?"

"Maybe. The thing is, if there are minerals in the stream bed, they'll show up right here, in the inside of this bend. It's where sediment would be deposited, and anything heavy that came up through the aquifer would be deposited right there because the water would lose force and drop what it's carrying."

"So you're saying you want to go out there and dig around?" Mack asked skeptically.

"Sure, why not?"

"Because there could be nothing."

"Or it could be the key to everything. What if someone discovered something out there? Maybe they didn't have the money to buy the land before I scooped it up. But if they scare me off, people might think twice before buying it from me, and maybe then they can get the ranch for a song, and whatever is out there would be theirs for the taking. We've eliminated the people who'd most likely want the land for the water. So it's worth a shot to see if someone might want it for a different reason."

"If you think so. I'm willing to go out there with you and take a look." Hell, what would it hurt? He didn't believe there was anything out there at all. In this drought, the water was the most valuable commodity there was, and if they didn't get rain soon, even the springs would begin to run dry. "We can take a look tomorrow."

"Okay," Brantley said and took the plot map. "I'll get out of your way."

"You're fine. I'm not getting anywhere very fast on this."

"I know you think this is a wild goose chase," Brantley said. "And you don't have to go with me. I can do this on my own."

Mack narrowed his eyes. "You sure as hell will not." He stood quickly and nearly knocked over the chair. "You've already been shot at, and I'm pretty sure you've been watched and followed. If you think I'm letting you go out there alone with little cover, you're crazy. I'm not particularly keen about going out there at all, but you damn well aren't going alone. I wonder if there's an army somewhere I can rent."

"Mack... I...." Brantley looked taken aback at Mack's protectiveness.

"I don't particularly like it, but it could be worth a look. There has to be some reason for all of this, and like you said, we've pretty much eliminated the water-rights angle. And you've helped Erickson out anyway. Something is going on that we don't know enough about, so we can see if there's anything there."

"Okay. I'm going to take a look and see what's been found in the area in the past. Maybe that will give us a clue." Brantley turned to leave the office, but Mack stopped him with both hands on Brantley's shoulders, then wheeled him around, kissing him possessively, taking what he wanted.

"I will not let anything happen to you."

Brantley shivered as Mack deepened the kiss, enfolding him into his arms. Mack pushed Brantley back until he reached the wall. Mack stifled a smile as more of his weight settled against Brantley. It was heady knowing he could buckle Brantley's knees with a kiss. Someone walked by the office, footsteps tapping on the floor, but he ignored it and Brantley did as well. Mack was too intent on kissing Brantley's breath away to stop now.

Once Mack pulled back, Brantley blinked a few times as though his mind was trying to make sure it had been real. The tingling on his lips reinforced to Mack that he'd just kissed him within an inch of his life, possessively, and he was damn proud of it.

"Mack…," Brantley breathed.

Mack didn't move away, staring intently into Brantley's eyes. "I have to know. Was last night just a sex thing for you?"

Brantley shook his head.

"Good. Fucking good. Because it wasn't for me either. So if we go out there, you'll do this my way and without argument. I said I'd do my best to keep you safe, and you damn well better do your part."

"Why are you acting like a bear with a thorn in its paw?" Brantley demanded.

"Because I don't want to lose what I just found," Mack answered and then backed away farther, his hands falling away from where he'd held Brantley's shoulders to the wall.

"When are we going?"

"Tomorrow," Mack reminded him. "If there's something out there, we need to know, and if there's not, then we're back to the drawing board."

CHAPTER 6

BRANTLEY WAS still in a bit of a daze when Mack drove them to his place. "Are you going back to work?"

"No. I can only stare at the same damn thing for so long, and I'm not going to get anything else out of it." He growled. "I hate that this guy is always one step ahead of us." Mack's knuckles went white from his grip on the wheel.

"Calm down. This guy is going to make a mistake, and then you'll catch him. It's as simple as that."

"Yeah. But what if someone else gets killed before he does? What if it's you?" Mack glanced over after pulling up at a stop sign.

"He wants something from me," Brantley explained. "I know it in my gut. He wants me alive for some reason. But he also doesn't want to tell us why."

"Which leads you to believe there's more to it than we thought about your land? What if he's trying to soften you up for money?"

"No," Brantley said, turning slightly on the seat so he could see Mack better. "This guy is focused on his goal. You thought he had training, and I think you're right. He's also got a certain level of discipline. He definitely wants something, and it has to do with me, so he wants me alive." He was fairly sure of that, just as he was sure that the sheriff taking an interest in him and offering extra protection wasn't in this guy's game plan. "He thought it would be easy to scare me away."

"So this guy doesn't know you very well."

Brantley nodded. "Nope, and I think that could be another clue. Though there aren't many people in town who do, so that isn't particularly helpful."

Mack pulled through the intersection and drove the rest of the way home in silence. "Something's wrong. I never leave the side door open," he said as he pulled into the drive. He got out of the car and went into cop mode. It would have been sexy if Brantley's ears weren't ringing with the blood that coursed through him. "Stay down and out of sight," Mack said, but Brantley ignored him, following right behind.

"I'll be damned if someone is going to catch me by surprise," Brantley hissed and stayed close.

Mack scanned the garage, gun in his hand, ready to fire. No one jumped out or started shooting, and they stepped cautiously through the garage toward the door to the house. It stood open, the jamb splintered. Mack continued forward, and Brantley still expected someone to jump out and start shooting at any second. No dogs came rushing toward them, and that in itself was a bad sign. The pack always greeted them when they came in the house.

"Dad," Mack ground between his teeth, and Brantley stifled a gasp. If anything happened to Lew because of him, he'd never be able to forgive himself. Mack pushed the door open farther and cautiously made his way inside. The kitchen looked normal.

"Mack!" Lew called.

"It's me," Mack answered. "Are you hurt?"

"No," Lew called as they continued through the house. "I'm in the bathroom."

"Stay here," Mack said to Brantley. "I want to check the rest of the house." He hurried away, and Brantley listened as every door was opened and closed. "It's clear," Mack eventually said, and Brantley joined him at the bathroom door.

Lew sat on the floor, back against the tub, his chair tipped on its side. A gun rested on his lap.

"You help Dad. I'm going to check out back," Mack said, and then he left.

"Do you always take a gun to the bathroom with you?" Brantley asked as he lifted the chair back onto its wheels.

"With all this brouhaha going on, I've taken to carrying one when I'm alone. If people will shoot at you and cut my son's brakes, I fully intend to be able to defend myself."

94

Brantley lifted Lew back into his chair. "What happened?"

"I was on my way here when I heard someone break down the door. I shut myself inside, and when I heard him outside the door, I said that I had a gun and that I'd just as soon blow his brains out. I expected the asshole to fire through the door or something, but after a while, I heard footsteps again and then silence until you got home. Of course I was stuck on the floor because I was in such a damned hurry, I tipped the dang chair."

"What do you think he wanted?" Brantley asked, as the dogs came rushing in.

"The dogs were out back and aren't hurt," Mack said as he stepped into the bathroom.

The dogs got their attention and reassurance before wandering back out, probably to check on the contents of their bowls.

"I think he wanted me. This asshole saw a guy in a wheelchair and thought I was easy pickings. He'd probably have kidnapped me to get whatever it is that he wants."

"Maybe this is another of his scare tactics," Brantley said. "Or he's becoming more desperate and is escalating and trying to ramp up the pressure." He leaned on the vanity to keep from falling. "Not that it matters. This is all because of me, and he came in here and could have hurt Lew because of me." He turned to Mack. "I can't live with that. If he wants the ranch and whatever's on it, he can have it. I'll leave town, and he can take whatever he wants. If it's water, gold, minerals, what the hell ever, he can have it." Brantley's arm shook. "I came here to try to find a new life, one with some peace and quiet, something closer to the earth and away from the politics and backbiting of the city."

"Brantley," Mack said. "I am going to find this guy."

"You better believe he is," Lew added, banging his fist on the arm of his chair. "This is a good place to live, and the people here are better than this."

"Are they? I've been verbally abused by two of my neighbors, and other than you, Mack, and Julie, not a single person has been the least bit friendly. I understand New York. Yeah, I can't do what I did before, but who cares. I can go back to what I know. At least there I know where the knives are coming from, and they don't tend to use real ones." He turned and left the bathroom, going to the guest room he'd been using. He sat on the edge of the bed, shaking. Brantley half expected Mack to come in to try to talk him out of it. But no one joined him, not for quite a while.

"Is that what you really want to do?" Mack asked, after knocking on the doorframe. "I have a friend who does carpentry—he'll fix the door. And I checked through the house. Other than that, you'd never know anyone was here."

"So." Brantley looked up from his shoes. "I should go."

"No, you shouldn't," Mack countered. "You're stronger than this, and you can't let him win."

"Is that all?" Brantley asked. "I should stay because of some male-ego thing about winning."

"No!" Mack said more loudly. "You should stay because I like you and want to get to know you. I thought I'd be alone and then I find you… with a dead body, of all things. How romantic is that?" He threw his arms in the air. "I meant I found someone I cared about along with a dead body. That has to be one of the most unlikely things in the history of the world. But I did, and you brought some sun to my life."

"He's been a complete pain in the ass for years," Lew interjected from the hallway.

"Dad, I'm trying to tell Brantley that he's special to me."

"Well, you're doing a shit job of it, son. Just say what's in your heart, and none of that flowery crap. It doesn't suit you."

Mack vibrated with suppressed laughter, and Brantley had to stop himself from laughing.

"I'd miss your dad if anything happened to him," Brantley said.

"I would too, but…." He turned toward the door. "Right now I'm wondering just what kind of a pain in the ass he can be."

A loud humph emanated from the hall, and then, after a few seconds, the television in the living room came on.

Mack turned back to him, this time with warmth and even a touch of worry in his dark eyes. "I don't want you to go. I just found you and I don't want to be alone again."

"But your dad… you could have lost your family because of me. Hell, I could have…. Lew is a great guy, and he could have been hurt…." Brantley swallowed hard. "Or worse, because of me. Dang it." He wiped his eyes. "I told myself I wasn't going to do this shit."

Mack leaned closer and hugged him tightly, rubbing his back. "I think we could have something special," he whispered.

"Oh God," Brantley breathed and held Mack right back. He had not come out here to find a guy, and then after all this shit, here he was. Mack was strong, manly, sexy as hell, and he could be caring and even understanding. But he feared that because of him, Mack could lose not just his life, but his dad.

"I know. It hit me all at once." Mack backed away. "If we really want to put an end to this and be safe again, then we have to stop running scared and try to catch this fucker." He slid his warm hand around the back of Brantley's neck. "But that could put you in danger, and that's the one thing I've been trying not to do."

"You mean use me as bait somehow?"

"Yes, that's what I meant, and no, I am not going to do it." Mack's intensity sent warmth through him. "I don't know how we're going to do it yet, but we will catch this man. I know there's something I'm missing, and I need to look at this problem differently, but damn it, it keeps escaping me." He shivered, and Brantley hoped he was all right. "I don't show weakness well. I'm expected to be strong, but I nearly lost my father today."

"Of course you're scared. That's enough to unsettle anyone."

"It is, but I'm supposed to stay in control. It's my job to keep everyone in this town safe, and I couldn't even do that for my dad, in my own home." Mack stood and paced the room. "Maybe I should join you in New York."

"Bullshit." Brantley's bout of self-pity seemed to have come to an end. "If you aren't going to let me run away, then you can't either. If this guy is going to be caught, then we need to do it together. As you said, there's something we're missing, and maybe we'll find part of that at the stream tomorrow."

"Mack!"

"I'll be right there, Zeb," Mack said. "I called him to take a look at the house. I'm getting too emotionally involved to be impartial, and there might be something I missed."

"Then let's go see," Brantley said. Mack had confided in him, and Brantley figured that was as close to a declaration of love as he was going to get. Not that he'd been gushing with sentiment, but it had felt good. Even after what had happened, it still made Brantley feel like he might have a place here, like he might have found a family of sorts.

Mack left the room, and Brantley followed. Mack went through to the back door with Zeb, while Brantley sat on the edge of the sofa nearest Lew. "Are you okay?"

"Yes. Mad as a wounded bobcat. That bastard came in my house, our house, as bold as he pleased. He knew Mack wasn't home and that I was alone. He yelled it as soon as he came in the door. Sucker didn't expect that I'd have a gun, though. I was ready to shoot him through the bathroom door, let me tell you."

"But he didn't get to you?"

Lew turned away from the television. "He didn't hurt me. But if I find out who the hell that is, I'm going to wring his damn neck and then run over his nuts with my chair." He banged his hand on the chair again. "Sometimes I hate being in this thing. If I were whole, I could have blown his ass away. Instead, I hid in the fucking bathroom."

Brantley had known that would bother Lew. "You did what was right, and if you think about it, you know it too. It's more important that you're here in one piece than if you'd have taken him on and ended up hurt or worse." Hesitantly, he touched Lew's hand, more to get his attention than anything else. "You've been very nice to me, and I'd never forgive myself if something happened to you."

"I suppose you're right," Lew said without pulling his hand away.

"Mack would be lost without you."

Lew shook his head slowly. "I think my son would be lost without you."

It was way too soon for things like that, and Brantley wasn't sure that was true anyway. "I don't know about that."

"Watch how he watches you. You do the exact same thing to him. I see it all the time. You have to know that I don't care that you're a man. My son is who he is. I told you that. So follow your heart, and maybe he'll do the same." Lew sighed a little. "He takes after his mother. She was a woman who lived in her head. She thought things over and made decisions based upon what she thought was right, but in the end, it was her heart that betrayed her. She needed to be with her people, but she ignored that need and it cost her dearly. If I had understood at the time, it might have changed things. But I was young and stupid."

"Brantley," Mack called, and he stood.

"Do what you think is right for both parts of yourself," Lew said. It seemed very strange to be having this conversation, and Brantley wasn't quite sure what had prompted it for Lew. But it was certainly nice to know they had his support.

"Look at this," Mack said as he approached, but Brantley didn't see anything. "Come over here and look in the light."

Brantley went over and took a look. "It's a boot print in the rug."

"Exactly. His feet were wet, and he stepped on the rug in his huge, heavy boots, leaving an indentation. It probably won't last long."

"How do we get a picture or something of it?"

"That's what we're trying to figure out. We don't have the money for fancy equipment."

"Turn on the flash on the camera. It will flood the area with light," Brantley said, and Zeb did as he asked and handed it to Brantley. He took it and got into just the right position and began taking pictures. When he was done, they looked at them on the screen.

"That one is pretty good," Zeb said.

"So is that one," Mack agreed. "Maybe we can figure out the kind of boot it is and who might have bought them."

Brantley heard the excitement in Mack's voice. Maybe this was the break they'd been hoping for. "I suppose we can try to match treads, but I'm assuming this isn't like on television, where they have databases for this type of stuff."

"That's true. We'll need to do this the old-fashioned way," Mack said. "Zeb, I want you to stay here with my dad until Brantley and I get back. I'm going to print this out as large as I can, and then Brantley here needs to go shopping for a real pair of boots rather than those fancy things he got in New York."

Brantley wanted to smack Mack, but he growled instead.

"I saw those boots, remember? They're something else," Zeb said.

Damn it, even Zeb was teasing him now. "There's nothing wrong with my boots. I got them at a very fashionable place and… shit." He wasn't going to win this, and he knew it.

"You need a real pair of work boots that will help support your feet. Not look like something from a fashion plate, especially tomorrow. Besides, we're on a hunt for a special kind of boot." Mack brought Brantley's thinking back to where it should be. "I'm going to my office to print these pictures, and then we'll get going." He turned to Zeb. "I contacted Frank, the carpenter we use. He's going to come out and remove the old jamb and replace it. We'll put it into evidence, along with the rug, and make sure Dad stays safe. This asshole broke into my house, and I'll be damned if he's going to do it again."

"What if he does come back?" Zeb asked.

"Take him into custody or shoot him, if necessary. But be careful. This guy has murdered someone, and he won't hesitate to do it again. He has nothing to lose," Mack said flatly. Then he left, clomping down to his office.

"So," Zeb began nervously. "You and the boss?"

Brantley didn't quite know what to say, so he simply nodded. He didn't know how Mack would classify what they were, and it was safer to let him do any explaining to his deputies.

"It's cool." Zeb gave him a slightly nervous smile.

"Thanks." Brantley was worried about how people would feel about him, but even halfhearted acceptance wasn't condemnation and he'd take that.

Mack returned with copies of the pictures and handed the camera back to Zeb. "Call me if anything happens." He led Brantley out to his truck. "I want to get there before the mercantile closes for the night. If the boots were bought in town, it was there. They have a full line of hunting gear, and that's what these look like to me."

Brantley climbed into the cab, and they barely had the doors closed before Mack was moving.

"Zeb asked about us," Brantley said as he fastened his seat belt. "While you were printing the pictures. He seemed okay, if a little uncertain. I wasn't sure what to say."

"How so? You could have told him whatever you wanted." Mack sped down the residential street, only slowing when they reached the main drag of town.

"I didn't know what to tell him. I don't know what we are to each other." Brantley hoped Mack would give him a thought as to what they were or at least how he thought others should think of them.

Mack pulled the truck into the lot at the mercantile and turned into an angled parking space. "You're my boyfriend, unless you don't want to be."

Brantley smiled and patted Mack's knee. "Okay, then. I can deal with that."

"Come on, sweetheart." Mack checked his watch. "They close in half an hour."

They got out of the truck and went inside. Mack seemed to have lost his urgency, but Brantley figured that was an act so the shopkeeper wouldn't know what he was up to.

"Hey, Greg," Mack said as he greeted the kid behind the counter. "You the only one working tonight?"

"Hey, Sheriff," Greg said. "Yeah. Dad's upstairs. Is this the new guy that bought the Richardson place?"

"Yes. This is Brantley. He's here from New York and, well, he needs some real boots."

"Everyone keeps giving me crap about mine," Brantley groused.

Greg shook Brantley's hand. "Sorry about all the stuff that's been happening to you. That isn't how things are here usually."

Brantley thanked him. "So you aren't part of the town who thinks I killed Renae," he said flatly.

"You wouldn't be out with the sheriff if you were. Besides, there weren't many people in town who thought very much of Renae. She was always nice when she came in here, but most people didn't like her, especially the women." Greg locked the register and came around the counter. "The boots are over here." He led the way to the side of the store. "I don't have every size out here, so if there's something you like, let me know and I can get your size."

"Thanks, Greg," Brantley said while Mack began looking.

Once Greg went back to his post, Mack pulled out the images he'd placed in his inside pocket and handed one to Brantley.

"I'm supposed to close in twenty minutes, but take your time," Greg called.

"Appreciate it," Mack called back and kept looking. There weren't that many different kinds of boots, and they quickly went through what was on the shelf with no luck. "Shit," Mack swore softly. "I was hoping we'd get a lead with this."

"Are things ever that easy?" Brantley asked.

"Not with this case, obviously." Mack put away the picture and blew air between his lips. He turned to leave, and Brantley took one last look through the display.

"Greg, what are those?" he asked, pointing to an unboxed pair of boots at the top of the display.

"We got some of those in by mistake. Dad was really pissed. They're super expensive, and they've been here a while."

"I like them," Brantley said, and Greg got a step stool and brought them down. Brantley took the pair and looked them over the way a purchaser would before turning them over. "What do you think, Mack?" He caught Mack's gaze for a few seconds, forgetting about the boots until Mack took them from him.

"I really like these. They're very well made, and the leather is really nice," Mack said.

"We've had them for two years, and we've only sold a few pairs. I can give you a good price if you want 'em," Greg said happily. "What size do you take?"

"Eleven," Brantley said, and Greg hurried away. "Looks like these are the boots."

"Yeah, and there can't be many people willing to spend five hundred dollars on a single pair of boots," Mack said, and Brantley nodded his agreement.

"I don't have an eleven, but these are cut differently, so I brought a ten and a half and a twelve. Usually boots are sized a little bigger." Greg handed Brantley the boxes, and he pulled off his sneakers and tried on the boots.

The ten and a half fit perfectly. "I'll take these," he told Greg happily, then pulled off the boots and put his sneakers back on.

Greg took the boots to the counter, and Brantley handed him his credit card.

"Not many people have ones like these, huh," Brantley said as he waited for Greg to complete the sale.

"Nope. I think Mr. Winters bought a pair. He's a vet and needs really good boots. He also has foot problems, and these are the boots for that. Dad sold a few pairs a while back, but that was about it."

"Do you know who he sold them to?" Mack asked.

"Nope. They've been here a while. Is it important?"

Mack nodded. "I'm afraid it is."

Greg finished the sale, and while Brantley signed the slip, Greg pulled out his phone. "Hey, Dad, the sheriff is here, and he wants to talk to you. I sold a pair of those Lucchese boots, and he wants to know who else bought a pair. I'm going to put him on." He handed the phone to Mack, who listened a few minutes and then handed the phone back.

"He doesn't remember. But he said he'd go through the records. He knows he sold a pair to Mr. Richardson, but that doesn't do us any good."

"Does this have to do with Renae's murder?" Greg asked.

"I can't answer that question, but thank you for your cooperation, and for your own safety, I would very much appreciate if you kept our conversation to yourself."

Brantley figured Mack was being a little harsher than necessary in order to keep his interest in the boots out of the rumor mill. "Thanks for your help," Brantley said as he slid the box with his new boots off the counter.

"Thank you, and you can count on me." Greg walked them to the door and let them out. He locked the door behind them, and Brantley hurried to the truck and got in.

"I hate being out in the open," he said as soon as they were in the truck, with his boots on the bench seat next to him. "I keep wondering if I'm being watched. There have been times when I can feel eyes on me but I don't see anyone. But the hair on the back of my neck stands on end, and I know someone is there."

"Did you feel it now?" Mack asked. "Never ignore those feelings. They are a holdover from when we were more primitive and needed them for survival in case we were being stalked by predators or hunters."

"Not this time. But I have in town. Not before the shooting in the diner. I have at the ranch, which pisses me off. I don't feel safe in my own home."

"You will. We're getting closer, and this guy is feeling it. If we're being watched, then he knows we've been talking to the neighbors and that we have to be eliminating possible people. He knows we'll be closing in on him. And maybe with the break-in, he thinks we're closer than we really are." Mack drove more slowly on the way back than he had on the way there.

"What I don't understand is why the guy doesn't just leave? He's shooting people and at people. By and large the town is looking for him. It isn't just you and me. He scared a lot of people with that shot through the window, and they have a right to be angry. Why stay?"

Mack pulled to a stop. "Because he wants something."

"Yes. But he has to know by now that he isn't going to get it. I'm not going to be scared away. That isn't going to happen. This town is my new home, and I'll be damned if I'm going to give it up because of some freak with a gun." Brantley clenched his fists as pride and backbone took over. He wasn't going run like some child.

"I'm glad." Mack flashed him a smile, then resumed driving. "I like that you want to stay. Is there any particular reason?" He suddenly had a touch of doubt in his voice.

"I like it here. The open space, and as I've gotten to know the people, they seem good and not quite what I originally thought. I wasn't exactly expecting that." Brantley smirked. "And there's a certain sheriff who swooped in to help keep me safe and who's becoming important to me." He sat back in the seat, keeping a little low.

They pulled into Mack's drive and into the garage. The lights were on and there was a carpenter repairing the back door. "Frank," Mack said happily. "I appreciate you coming out quickly."

"No problem at all." He set down his tape measure. "Someone has balls if they're going to break into your house. What's going on?"

"We're still trying to figure it out, but I believe it's someone's fear campaign. I don't know if we'll know until I catch this guy. But I will." Mack let Frank finish his work and continued inside.

Zeb sat with Lew. "It's been quiet," Zeb said as he set a mug on the table and stood. "I'm going to check in at the station and then head on home."

"Thanks for everything," Mack said.

"Did you find what you needed?" Zeb asked.

"In a way," Mack said as Brantley set his box with his boots on the sofa and pulled it open. "Our break-in suspect wore boots like these." He turned them over and handed one of the photograph copies to Zeb. "Greg at the mercantile said they haven't sold many pairs. Richardson had a pair, but that doesn't help us. They said they sold a few other pairs a while ago, but can't remember who bought them. They were going to try to find out, but I don't think they'll get anywhere."

"Denny Beltz," Zeb said, turning the boots over in his hands. "He has a pair. I remember seeing them."

"Julie's husband?" Brantley asked. He remembered hearing his name on his first visit. "He's away at Reserves until the end of the week." That certainly didn't help them. "So that leaves us nearly nowhere."

"There must still be someone else who has a pair," Mack said, exasperation clear in his voice.

"I'll take off and see you in the morning," Zeb said, and Mack saw him out.

Once he was gone, Mack called into the station to check in, and Brantley settled in the living room.

Frank finished his work, and Mack took care of him and turned off the outside lights before joining them once again. It was clear that Mack was just as keyed up as Brantley was. They both sat on the sofa, Brantley's leg bouncing. He was nervous as hell.

"I'm going to bed," Lew said, and Mack wheeled him down the hall, not returning for a while.

"He's really shaken up. I know he doesn't want to talk about it or seem weak, but I don't know how much sleep any of us are going to get tonight."

"Should one of us stay up, just in case?" Brantley asked. "I can rest out here."

"I've been wondering the same thing. I thought my house would be safe, but that doesn't seem to be the case." He sighed. "You go on to bed, and I'll sit up out here. It isn't like I'm going to sleep much, and you might as well try to rest." Mack left and returned in a T-shirt and workout shorts, carrying a blanket.

He knew this wasn't the time, but Brantley still had difficulty taking his gaze off the way Mack stretched the fabric of that shirt nearly to the limit. Mack was a stunning man, and now that he had his hair loose, he was even more impressive. His Native American heritage came out even more in his features. "Okay," Brantley said absently, his gaze shifting downward. He did his best not to leer but couldn't help it. Mack's bulge was impressive, as was the way his legs stretched his shorts. "I should try to sleep," he agreed and left the room. If he stayed, he wasn't going to be able to restrain himself, and since Lew had just gone to bed, Brantley jumping Mack in the living room probably wasn't the best idea.

Brantley said good night and hurried to the guest room. He got his kit and used the bathroom before returning to the bedroom and climbing under the covers in his boxers and an old concert T-shirt.

The house was quiet and dark. Brantley had expected Mack to stay up watching television, but it seemed he'd decided to try to rest as well. Every now and then Brantley heard the faint squeak of springs as Mack shifted out on the sofa.

Brantley lost track of how long he lay staring up at the ceiling. Minutes or hours, it was hard to tell. What he knew for sure was that he wasn't going to sleep. He was too nervous, and every sound in the house had him jumping just a little. Frustrated, he got up and wandered out to the living room.

Mack lay on his side on the sofa, facing out into the room. His eyes opened as Brantley approached, and he moved back, lifting the blanket. "I can't sleep either," he whispered.

There wasn't much room, but Brantley lay down. Mack nearly pushed him onto the floor as he removed the back cushions. Then he moved back. Brantley settled next to him, Mack's strong arm sliding right around him, his big hand settling on Brantley's belly.

Brantley closed his eyes and tried to sleep, but it seemed Mack had other ideas. Mack kissed the back of his neck and then teasingly licked the edge of his ear. Brantley shivered, and Mack slipped his hand under Brantley's T-shirt, stroking his stomach and occasionally sliding his hand upward, teasing his nipples. Brantley clamped his eyes closed and his lips together to keep from groaning. His cock pressed against his stomach, and every time Mack's fingers brushed the base of his belly, Brantley pressed his hips forward, silently willing Mack to go further, but he backed away time and time again.

"I know what you want," Mack whispered into his ear and then pressed his hips to Brantley's ass, his thick, hard cock pressed right to the crack. "I want it too." He backed away and then pressed Brantley's boxers down to expose his butt. Mack pressed his now bare cock to his ass, and Brantley swallowed hard, soaking in the heat. "Like that?"

"Yeah," Brantley breathed, about ready to grab Mack's hand and push it to his cock or else he was going to take matters into his own hand.

Mack muttered something about patience and continued his slow ministrations. Brantley quivered, hoping like hell he could keep quiet. Figuring it was better to make the most of this time rather than rush things, he stretched out, the soft fabric of the sofa sliding along his shoulder and side. Mack continued rubbing, and Brantley whimpered softly when Mack's fingers went south, finally touching him. He didn't apply much pressure, lightly grazing his fingers along Brantley's shaft and then over his balls.

The sensation was sublime, and he groaned before he could stifle it. He prayed Lew was asleep. He didn't want to wake him for a number of reasons, including the fact that the last thing he wanted was an interruption. "Don't stop," Brantley whispered into the dark room.

"I won't, sweetheart," Mack answered.

Brantley loved when Mack used that endearment. He hoped it was something Mack truly meant instead of just an affectation.

Mack grasped his shaft, stroking slowly as he sucked on Brantley's earlobe.

"God…." He moaned under his breath.

"You feel so damn good," Mack said softly, grinding his cock against Brantley's ass.

Damn, Brantley wanted to take this further. Instead, he held still and gave his pleasure over to Mack. There was something wonderful and freeing about letting go and giving Mack the control. It sounded selfish, but he loved that Mack cared enough to want him to be happy. It meant he was special and, well, it had been a long time since he'd felt that way.

Mack continued stroking him. "I want to slide inside you so bad," he breathed. "I want to feel your heat around me." Mack quivered and pressed into him harder.

Brantley clenched his cheeks, trying to add more pressure. His head spun as desire ramped up higher and higher, filling the room. Brantley wanted what Mack did, but there were no supplies here, so it was either move or make the most of it. He had no intention of stopping, and Mack gripped him harder as he worked his other arm beneath him. Brantley lifted himself up, and Mack held him in both arms, tightening his hug, driving Brantley completely out of his mind. He leaned back as Mack stroked and petted him, Brantley's insides coming to a boil as pressure built that he wouldn't be able to contain for long.

"Are you going to come for me? I wish I could see it. You look so amazing when you come. Your eyes almost glow, and your tongue sticks ever so slightly between your teeth." Mack gripped his cock hard but stopped stroking.

"Do I look dumb?" Brantley had never thought about how he looked during a moment like that.

"You look amazing, flushed and beautiful. I know I won't be able to see it, but I want to make you feel that way right now." Mack held him tighter, tweaking a nipple before gliding his finger along Brantley's cock with agonizing slowness.

Brantley shook with pent-up energy, pushing his hips forward and then back. "Mack, I…."

"Yeah, you do. I can feel you shaking. I know you're so close— so am I. If I slid into you, I'd spill before I even got inside." Mack sucked on his ear once again, and the last bit of control that Brantley clung to began slipping away. This was too much, and all he could do was give himself over to it. Mack gripped him tighter, stroking faster, sliding his cock along his ass.

Brantley didn't know where to put his attention. Everything felt too damn good, and his head spun in circles. Finally the cloud of sheer excitement became too much, and he let it take over, no longer fighting it. Mack stroked him slowly once again, sliding his fingers over the

109

top of the head. Hell, if Mack had pushed inside him, Brantley would have spilled a while ago, but Mack seemed to know exactly what would make him tumble, and he kept Brantley just this side of it.

Sweat broke out all over as the tide of energy inside grew higher and higher. He wanted to come more than anything in the world. All his attention was on Mack, where he touched him and how he played his body. Mack seemed to know everything he was going to do and how he was going to react before Brantley did it.

"Not yet," Mack breathed. "I'm going to drive you out of your mind, make you so hot that when you do come, you're going to feel like your head is going to split apart and your heart will leap from your chest." He stopped, and Brantley breathed through his open mouth to pull air into his lungs.

"How… what… are… you… going…."

"Shhh," Mack said. "You'll find out soon enough." Mack released him, and Brantley growled, instantly missing the heat and pressure of Mack's hand. "Raise your leg, sweetheart," he asked, and Brantley complied without thinking. Mack slid his fingers around and then pressed two inside him.

Brantley hissed at the invasion and then murmured incoherently when Mack gripped his shaft. Brantley knew he was completely wanton, greedy, and he needed all of it. Mack tightened his grip, stoking Brantley's cock while sliding his fingers in and out of him. There was no way in hell Brantley could take much of this. It was overwhelming and way over the top. His legs shook and his hands tingled, the sensation growing and sliding down his spine. Brantley clamped his eyes closed and held his breath, hoping for that tiniest bit more of sensation. He gasped, and Mack stroked just a hair faster, and it was enough. The pressure inside blossomed and grew to the point where it was more than he could handle. Brantley stilled completely, withdrawing into his head as he came over Mack's hand. Everything receded until it was only him and Mack, nothing else. He stilled and floated in Mack's arms. It took him a few seconds before things came back to him.

"I'm going to need to get something to clean us up," Mack said.

Brantley hummed and stayed still. It wasn't a minute more before he realized he was wet both front and back, and that moving either way meant a dose of cool dampness. He raised the blanket, and Mack slowly got up, climbed over him, and returned with a towel that Brantley used for a quick cleanup.

"This is a little silly," Brantley said as he wiped his backside. "There are two perfectly good beds, and if either of us is going to be worth anything in the morning, we'll need some sleep." He pulled up his boxers and took Mack's hand, still holding the towel. Without another word, he led Mack down the hall.

Mack took the towel and tossed it in the hamper in the bathroom and then pushed open his bedroom door. They went inside, and Mack left the door open. "I want to hear if anything happens."

Brantley pulled off his T-shirt, which was sticky in places, and followed Mack into bed. Instantly he was tugged close and held.

"You are special, I want you to know that," Mack said.

Special. Brantley had never thought of himself that way. He had things he was good at, but being special and dear to someone warmed him no end. "You're pretty amazing yourself," Brantley said and closed his eyes, patting Mack's hand on his belly, hoping the rest of the night would be quiet.

BRANTLEY WOKE to an empty bed. He heard soft voices in the house and quietly got up, walked across to the guest room, and closed the door. He noticed the bathroom was empty too, so he took the chance to shower and dress. When he opened the door, Mack stood outside, looking edible, and Brantley realized he might have missed a chance to see and feel a wet, shower-soaked Mack.

"I didn't want to wake you."

"I woke because I was getting a little cold, and a certain furnace wasn't next to me." Brantley grinned and stepped out of the way.

"Are you wearing that for our expedition this morning?" Mack tugged him closer, sliding an arm around his waist. "You look great in those jeans, but if we're going to do this, I don't want us to make a

111

spectacle of ourselves. I have some hunting clothes that we can wear. They're camouflage, and if someone is watching, that will make it harder for them to see us."

"Oh." Brantley barely heard what Mack said. His mind was on how close he was and how that was enough to get his head spinning a little and his body to run on overdrive.

"I'll clean up and bring you the clothes so we can change and go." Mack leaned closer still. "Though I'm tempted to take you back to bed and see if we could stay there for the rest of the day."

"I like that idea, but then we'll never get anything done." Brantley was about to chuck it all and figure out a way to get dirty so he could clean up with Mack, but instead he kissed him and then stepped away. "Go on. I'll be waiting for you."

"Dad is making a simple breakfast. He was asking when you'd be up. So go on through."

"He doesn't need to do that."

"My dad wants to be helpful. When he was first in the chair, I tried to do everything for him. It was wrong. He simply sat back and didn't cope. It wasn't until I stepped back and let him do for himself that he began to thrive again. So let him do what he can." Mack kissed him once again and then stepped into the bathroom, closing the door.

Brantley went out to the kitchen, and Lew got him some coffee and a plate of eggs and toast. Brantley thanked him and tucked in.

"I take it you worked up an appetite."

Brantley colored. Had Lew heard them? Brantley stared down at his plate, trying not to give anything away.

"Running all over the place with Mack, I mean. It's his job to follow up on cases."

"This one seems to take both of us," Brantley said. "And I think I like it. Well, except the part about people breaking in here and getting shot at." He took a bite of eggs. "These are really light and good." He sipped his coffee. "My old job involved ferreting out the solutions to puzzles, and I think I miss that."

"I'll be glad when this whole business is over and everything goes back to normal." Lew put a plate on his lap and brought it over, then set it on the table and slid into place. "Damn, I forgot my coffee."

Brantley got up to get it for him and set it on the table before sitting back down. "Is going back to the way things were so important?"

"Are you asking about you and Mack? Because that's one area where I'm glad things have changed. I want him to be happy."

"I hope that I—"

Lew threw back his head, laughing. "For the last four days, that boy has walked on air. And you seem to smile a lot as well."

"But I worry. What is everyone in the county going to think about having a gay sheriff? What if being with me costs Mack his job?"

"Mack is well thought of, and I don't think most people are going to give two hoots about who he sleeps with."

"It doesn't take many people to stir up anger and resentment. People want to feel safe and like they know their neighbors. Mack is a great sheriff and an incredible man, but… I don't want him to pay a price if he chooses to be with me."

Lew set his mug down. "There's always a price for everything."

"Yeah, but…." Brantley's argument died on his lips.

"I wish I could tell you how things will be, but I can't, and I don't know what will happen. I do know that you should let Mack decide what he wants to do and whom he wants to fight, because if there is a challenge for his job, Mack will fight for it. I know he will."

"But he shouldn't have to," Brantley said.

"He's a good sheriff, and you're right, he shouldn't, but if it comes to that, then let him make that decision." Lew finished his coffee as Brantley cleared the table. "I can tell what you're thinking," Lew said as he pushed away from the table. "Mack doesn't need someone to throw himself on his sword for him. He needs someone who will face whatever comes along with him. And believe me, that takes more strength than anything else."

"What does?" Mack asked as he came into the kitchen, dressed like a hunter from head to toe. His pants were a little baggy, but his shirt was tight and showed off his arms.

Brantley had never thought that camo could be sexy, but Mack definitely made it so.

"We were just talking," Lew said. "You going hunting?"

"Yeah. Brantley, I put your clothes in the bedroom," Mack said, and Brantley went down the hall to change.

He heard Mack and Lew talking as he went, but he couldn't make out what they were saying. He found the clothes on Mack's now-made bed and began to change. What Mack had left out was surprisingly comfortable. The pants and shirt were kind of big, but he made them work.

"What kind of shoes should I wear?" Brantley asked Mack as he came into the living room. He sat down, and the dogs all came over for attention. Lulu tried to jump in his lap, but he stopped her gently.

"Normally I'd say to wear the boots you got last night, but they might hurt your feet until they're broken in. Put on sneakers and bring along an extra pair, if you have them, in case you get wet," Mack explained as he pulled open the repaired back door and went out into the garage.

Brantley followed and helped Mack load some gear into his truck, and then they took off. "Have you given any thought to where we're going to park? I'm assuming we don't want to leave the truck at my ranch."

"Nope. There's a make-out spot along the creek. We'll park there and walk up the bed to the bend. That will be the best and least visible way. There's a path, so it shouldn't be too hard." Mack didn't seem to be taking the most direct route, and sure enough, they crossed the creek from the far side and then Mack turned off and down a narrow track before coming to a stop.

It was quiet when Brantley got out, with only the light sounds of birds and the gurgle of water over stones. This was why he'd moved out here. He wanted to be able to hear himself think rather than car horns and the rumble of the city that had never seemed to quiet, no matter the time of day or year.

Mack broke the silence by shutting his door and trudging toward the back of the truck. "Grab a bundle and let's get going. We have a few hours before it gets really hot, and if we're going to do this, we need to get it done." He grabbed some tools, and Brantley lifted out a mesh bag, then followed Mack down what seemed to be a path. "This doesn't get used much, so be careful and watch for limbs."

Thankfully, when they got closer to the creek, the path cleared and they could walk easily under the trees that flourished from the constant source of water.

"I used to come out here sometimes when I was a teenager," Mack said as they walked. "In the summer it was cooler and a great place to get away from parents."

"Did you use the make-out spot?" Brantley teased.

"Once or twice. But I was trying to figure shit out then. I gave being like everyone else a shot, but mostly I came out here to hang out and try to beat the heat."

"The stream sure is pretty. I hadn't had a chance to come out here yet," Brantley said, stopping for a second to watch the water. "My life in New York was always run, run, run. I wanted to be able to take it slower and enjoy life before it was gone."

"So you came here, but someone decided you were in their way."

"Exactly." He didn't want to go over what had happened again. Every time he thought about the events of the past few days, he wanted to pack up and go home. But he didn't. He was too stubborn, and he hoped now he had someone to stay here for. "Let's keep going."

Mack continued leading him down the path. "Don't get too close to the edge. The creek is always cutting into the ground, and it could cave in." He grabbed Brantley and pulled him away just as his foot threatened to slip off the edge.

"I get that." Brantley was more careful where he stepped after that.

"Also watch out for snakes. They usually stay near the water. Most likely they'll be sunning themselves, but keep your eyes open."

"You should have told me," Brantley said, stopping as he thought he saw a stick move.

Mack kept going. "They're more scared of you than you are of them. Just don't get too close and they'll go the other way," he said, but Brantley wasn't so sure and slowed down, looking more intently ahead and to the side. The last thing he needed was to get bitten by something poisonous. That would be just his luck. "We're almost there."

"Thank goodness," Brantley said and drew closer. At the bend in the creek, Brantley set down the gear and walked out onto a small lower-lying area. "This is where anything would be deposited."

"What are we looking for?" Mack asked. "This hardly seems like an area that would be rich in gold, and it isn't likely that the spring would bring up something so heavy." He stood on the side of the stream, looking back and forth.

"This area is made up of rolling hills, but in the past, these hills were higher—they've been worn down. Who knows what's been left behind?" Brantley had to agree with Mack that there wasn't likely to be anything here, but there had to be some sort of answer to this mystery, and he was damn well going to find it. "There is gold in the Black Hills just a few hundred miles away, so who knows?"

"Brantley, let's say there is gold here. Would there be enough to make it worth anyone's while? A few flakes doesn't mean there's enough to kill for." Mack pulled open the pack Brantley had brought down. "I just don't see this as anything that special. If the stream had its beginnings farther west, then it might carry sediment that could have something. But this is just a spring-fed stream."

"I know. But I'm running out of explanations, and I want to try to find something."

"All right," Mack agreed and handed him a pan. "You dig up the loose gravel from the stream. Any gold will be found in the finest sand, so pick out the bigger rocks and swish out the rest to get to the really fine sand. Then take a look and see if anything glimmers." He demonstrated and held up the sandy bottom, letting the water fan it out. "Nothing."

Brantley took a turn, and while he was clumsy at it, he managed to get down to the fine silt and also found nothing. No gold and nothing of interest. Only sand. Brantley knew it had taken people a long time to discover anything in the past, so he kept it up, moving a few feet in either direction, sometimes out farther into the stream and other times closer to where the water cut at one of the banks.

"Anything?" Mack asked after about an hour.

"No. Maybe this was the dumbest thing I've ever done," Brantley said, scooping up another pan. "It's only a stream, and they could be after anything."

"Or we could be on a wild goose chase," Mack grumbled and stood, stretching his back. "Now I know why they always show miners as grizzled old men. Really they were only thirty, but all this bending and stooping aged them fast."

"Tell me about it." Brantley did the same, looking up and down the bank. "We'll give it a few more minutes and then pack it in." He was sweating up a storm, his feet were wet, and the bugs were becoming vicious. There was likely nothing here. Whenever they took a possible step forward, it turned out to be nothing and they were right back where they started.

Brantley tried to find a good spot to get another sample, walking down the bank of the creek. He saw a spot that looked interesting toward where the creek began its turn. He stepped on a rock, and it turned under his foot, throwing Brantley off-balance. He flailed his arms to keep from falling in. Thankfully he didn't, but he stepped right into the creek's cold water. His shoe got sucked under a soft spot and, when he pulled it out, his foot came, but his shoe stayed in the mud. "Damn it," Brantley swore, and Mack laughed loud and hard as he came over. "I have to fish the damn thing out."

"I'll get it." Mack managed to bend over and retrieve the shoe, covered in mud. He washed it in the running water, getting most of the mud off, and then handed him the sopping shoe. "I know it isn't going to be comfortable, but put it on so you don't cut your foot on anything."

Brantley sat down on the edge of the bank and squeezed his wet foot into his shoe. God, it felt awful. He was ready to go back, but Mack went to work, so Brantley scooped some of the creek bed into his pan and began separating out the larger pieces. By the time he got to the smaller pieces, Brantley swirled the pan in the water and stopped as a glimmer caught his eye. He reached into the pan and pulled out a small nugget.

"Mack?" he called and held out his hand. "Is this what I think it is?"

Mack came over and stared at the nugget. He took it and turned it over in his hand a few times. "That's exactly what you think. There is gold here after all."

"Holy crap," Brantley said, staring at the nugget. "What the hell do I do now?"

"At least now we know what our shooter is after. He drives you off the land, buys it, or just comes out here while the land is empty and works this area to take what he can get. There isn't a way to trace gold, so eventually he melts it down and makes whatever money he can get for it."

"But who would do that?"

"Someone who needs money pretty badly. People will do just about anything for gold. They've killed, cheated, threatened, and God knows what else for it during the various rushes, and it looks like we have someone who's willing to kill for it now. Where exactly did you find it?"

"At the start of the bend. But who knows? It could be anywhere and I just got lucky."

"True. It could also be that the area has already been worked. Maybe our killer has been coming out here for a while. You never know. The stream can cover a lot of activity."

"What do we do from here?" Brantley asked.

"We keep quiet for now and use what we just found out to try to identify our man. We have a motive for someone wanting to drive you off and for Renae's death. She handled the sale of the land." Mack began packing up the equipment. "Imagine this. You have your eye on this place because you found a nugget or flake out here. It's been empty for a while, and you know the family is getting anxious to sell. There was talk that the property was going to go to auction."

"But I buy the place through Renae instead," Brantley supplied.

118

"Exactly. His plans are up in smoke unless he can drive you away. He finds out you're from the city. So he figures he can kill two birds with one stone. Maybe he already hated Renae, so he lured her out to the ranch, shot her, and then called it in when he saw you coming home. A little confusion and he has time to get away and an easy initial suspect. When you don't leave, he ramps up and takes a shot at you." Mack finished gathering the equipment and sat on a log at the edge of the creek bed. "Then he starts escalating. He's been watching you, and by connection, me. He tampers with my brakes and then eventually breaks into the house."

"I don't get the break-in. That seems like a big risk," Brantley said. "And it gave us a clue."

"But he showed that we aren't safe, and that's what he's trying to do. Make you feel vulnerable everywhere so you return to where you once felt safe. This guy is well trained and has left few clues." Mack stood. "Let's get back to the truck and out of here. It's getting hot, and we don't want to be spotted if we can help it." He picked up the bundle and was about to pick up the other one when he dropped the bundle on the ground. "You have great instincts."

"I do?"

"I never would have thought about coming out here to look. You did, and it turned out to be right."

"I'm glad I was, but we aren't any closer to finding out who's behind this."

"We are. We now have a clear motive, as well as other clues. Something is going to break very soon, I know it. And when it does, we'll have him." Mack stepped closer, leaned down, and kissed him. "There are so many things that surprise me about you."

"Is that good?" Brantley asked.

"It's amazing." Mack flashed a smile, his gaze as hot as the sun overhead. "Come on. Let's get back and out of these clothes." Mack picked up one bundle and Brantley got the other, and they walked back along the path.

When they were about halfway there, Brantley said, "Mack, we're being watched from somewhere." A cold zing went up his spine and settled at the base of his neck.

"I feel it too," Mack said softly, slowing down. "Don't rush. Think about what we want him to see. If we're being watched, then let's put on an act. It isn't likely he saw us by the creek. The growth is too thick around there."

"Okay."

"So we need to look disappointed," Mack said softly. "Don't rush, and keep your shoulders slumped a little. Make a big deal of taking off your shoe and throwing it in the back of the truck. You're frustrated and angry. Let him think his secret is safe."

"Why?"

"I'm not sure. But if we know something and he doesn't, then that could give us the upper hand." Mack continued, slowly trudging along. When he approached the truck, he heaved the bundle of tools in the back and leaned against the truck, gaze facing downward. Even Brantley began to think that he'd done something to disappoint Mack.

He tossed the bag of stuff in the back with a clatter and got his dry shoes, then took off the wet ones, cursing as he threw each one in the bed of the truck. "Let's get the hell out of here so we can dry off." He got in the truck and slammed the door. He waited, and Mack popped up on his side of the cab and then continued around.

"Start the engine and back out slowly. I want to make sure there are no puddles of fluid. Then we'll go back to town."

Brantley slid over, started the engine, and put the truck in reverse. He backed up, and then Mack got into the passenger seat. "Take us to the ranch. I want him to see us go there and look around."

"Why?"

"It's what he'd expect us to do. We're here, and it's logical for us to make sure everything is okay. We don't have to stay long."

"Okay." Brantley drove around to the front of the ranch and pulled into the drive. He slowly pulled up to the house, which looked the same. The door was still closed.

"Give me your house keys and stay here. I'm going to check the barn and the house. Then we can go in, and you can get anything else you need."

"Do you think we're getting close?"

"Yeah. I don't know why, though, but one small fact is going to tip us over the edge. I can feel it." Mack got out and closed the door.

Brantley locked the doors and put the truck in gear, ready to take off at a second's notice. He watched Mack go into the barn, then step out and walk slowly to the house. Mack went inside and, after a few anxious minutes, came back out. Brantley turned off the engine and pulled the brake. He got out and handed Mack the truck keys before going inside.

The house, his home, seemed strange to him. He hadn't spent much time there, but the house felt empty and lifeless. His furniture didn't look comfortable. It almost seemed as though it belonged to someone else. Brantley pushed all that from his head and went down to his bedroom. He grabbed a duffel bag and began filling it with a few additional changes of clothes. He looked through the room, but it was as he'd left it. The paint on the walls was someone else's, and it left him cold and wondering what in the hell he had expected to find out here.

"What's going on?" Mack asked.

Brantley turned to find Mack leaning against the doorframe. "Nothing," he answered and went back to packing.

"Bullshit. I've seen that look. You were a million miles away, or at least a few thousand."

"Actually, I wasn't." He scanned the room. "I was thinking about my room. This is where I'm supposed to live and sleep, but it feels strange to me." He was more at home in Mack's guest room than he was here in his own house.

"You weren't here very long," Mack reminded him.

"No. I remember being told once that a home is about the people who are there, rather than the building, and I think I forgot that. I moved out here thinking I could build a new home. But this isn't it." Brantley closed the duffel and set it on the bed. "I mean, this could be it, but not if I'm alone here. Then it's just a house on a large piece of land." He lifted the bag and left the room, passing Mack along the way. "I think we can go now."

"Okay." Mack followed him. "If you want to make this a home, then you could."

"How? Convince you and Lew to pull up stakes and move out here?" Brantley asked and immediately realized what he'd said. "There's nothing here. My life in New York was work and little else. I came out here to change my luck and start fresh, but I fell into the same rut, except without the work."

"You haven't been here that long. Once this is over, have a cookout and invite everyone you know. Fill your house with people and fun, and your barn with horses or whatever you want. You could also fill your fields with cattle and life. That's the heart of a ranch, and I think why this life is so appealing."

"Maybe you're right." He noticed Mack didn't comment on his slip.

"Though I do agree that filling this house with people who care for you would be special." Mack's mischievous smile lit up the living room.

"Have you ever thought about living on a ranch?"

"I used to, and I think I'd like to. But maybe it's a little early for conversations like this. I mean, we've known each other for less than a week. Let's take things one step at a time." Mack reached out and yanked him close, and Brantley dropped his bag to the floor. "I realize how what I just said sounded, and while I'm not ready to set up housekeeping, I doubt you are either at this point. But I have no intention of just letting you go." Mack leaned in, tugging Brantley even closer.

Brantley tensed in anticipation and put his arms around Mack's neck, pressing tightly to his hard body. In his fantasies the men were always big, strong, and dark, like Mack, with eyes that burned for him. Brantley had always doubted that his dream man actually existed, and that even if he did find him, he'd be interested in him. Mack certainly was, judging by the bulge that pressed to his and the way his lips took possession of Brantley's. Damn, Mack was powerful and smelled like fresh air and sunshine sitting on top of riotous pheromones. He made Brantley's head spin.

He kissed like a dream, the perfect combination of force and gentleness. Brantley held tight, returning Mack's kiss and wishing like hell he'd move them back into his room. The bed was only a few feet away, and he was ready to be taken—for Mack to make love to him, full-on, without reservations.

Mack pushed him against the wall, and Brantley *oomph*ed but didn't pull away from Mack's talented lips. He was on fire, and thinking was something he'd gladly left behind. Everything pushed him to this man and damn any consequences.

"Sweetheart, we should get home."

"I know," Brantley agreed and cut off Mack's next words by pushing against him, taking what he wanted.

Mack encircled him in his arms, lifting him off the ground, and Brantley wrapped his legs around Mack's waist.

"Take me into the bedroom," Brantley demanded, and Mack carried him back through the door, then laid him on the bed, huge hands supporting his ass.

"I'm going to do what we didn't last night."

"Fuck yes!" Brantley groaned and lay back, pulled his shirt over his head, and opened his pants.

Mack pulled Brantley's pants down to his ankles and yanked off his shoes before pulling his pants off and onto the floor. Brantley thought he might have heard some stitches give way in the process, but he was too far gone to really care. Mack pulled off his shirt and pushed down his pants, then rummaged in the nightstand for a condom. "Fuck yes, prelubed." He rolled it on and leaned over Brantley, dark eyes burning. "This is going to be fast, but I need you right the hell now." Mack fumbled as he found some lube, slapped it on Brantley's opening, and then pushed in. Mack shook as he sank deeper into him.

Brantley groaned and held the edge of the mattress. He was afraid he'd fly apart any second and had to hold it together. The stretch and burn were heady. They lasted seconds, and then he was full and ready to rocket to Mars.

Mack pressed deep, holding still for only a matter of seconds.

"Holy Jesus, God," Brantley swore as Mack lowered his body a little and sent him to orbit. Fucking was one thing. Brantley had fucked and been fucked before, but with Mack it was different, so very different. Every touch and sensation was heightened and special. When Mack touched him, it wasn't about how fast he could get off, but to show that he cared. And being cared about was one of the things Brantley had been looking for without really knowing it, until Mack stepped into his life.

Mack leaned over him, their kisses sloppy and wonderful. Mack filled the entire room with energy, and Brantley fed off it, needing that like parched earth needs the rain. "You are special," Mack whispered.

"And you fill my world," Brantley said in return, holding Mack's gaze with his and then pulling him down. He needed to feel the connection between them, and Mack seemed more than happy to oblige. Brantley knew he was falling for Mack, hard, but he still wasn't ready to say the words. Or maybe he was waiting for Mack to say them first.

At the moment none of that mattered. Brantley was on fire, and he stroked himself to the rhythm Mack set, closed his eyes, and readied himself for the ride of his life. "Mack," Brantley cried.

"I know," Mack growled, adding to the sheer passion between them.

Brantley held off as long as he could before tumbling over the edge, spilling onto his chest and belly. Mack followed shortly behind him, throbbing inside Brantley's passage until his eyes crossed.

Mack stilled, and Brantley kept his eyes closed. He wanted to see Mack, but he still had the feeling that if he didn't close them, his eyes were going to pop from his head because of the pressure. The pressure subsided quickly, replaced with floating on clouds, the euphoria that came from being close to Mack. Brantley knew it was only a physical rest period, but he reached for Mack and tugged him down, holding him tightly, like his world depended on it.

He was gone, very far gone, and in so much trouble. Brantley had already given his heart to Mack. The knowledge filled him with both happiness and fear. Brantley didn't know how in hell he was going to keep Mack happy. He was this skinny guy, and Mack was hunky and gorgeous and could have any guy he wanted.

"What are you thinking about?" Mack asked. "You screwed your face up like you'd just eaten something sour."

"Nothing," Brantley said. "I was just…." He sighed. "I was wondering what you could possibly see in me." He stroked Mack's arm and groaned softly when their bodies separated. He should simply keep his mouth shut and learn to take things as they came.

"You do know it's possible to think too much, right?" Mack said and kissed him gently, his lips tugging playfully at Brantley's. "And you're about to turn that into an Olympic sport."

"Why do you say that?" Brantley asked, sitting up, and Mack moved back.

"We just made love, and you're worrying about God knows what," Mack said, clearly hurt.

Brantley blinked, ignoring Mack's tone. "Made… love. You love me?"

"Yes," Mack said as though he were surprised. "I know it seems fast, and maybe it is, I don't know. I'm no expert on these things."

"I wish I were," Brantley muttered and then forgot about everything else. "I have this history with men that's rocky and barren. I never had much luck… until now." Brantley let himself believe that maybe his fortune in that area of his life was changing. "And for the record, I'm falling in love with you too."

"I hate to interrupt this moment, but we should get back. I don't like leaving Dad alone, and I should go in and see if I can figure out what's going on." Mack straightened up. He pulled up his pants and half waddled out of the room, then returned with a cloth from the bathroom. Mack gently cleaned him up and then kissed him. "I have to tell you that I'd like nothing more than to spend the entire day right here with you."

125

"I'd like the same thing, but I know you can't." Brantley stretched, his muscles deliciously sore, watching Mack as he dressed.

Brantley sank deep in his own thoughts. Under some of the worst and most frightening circumstances in his life, he had found someone special. Maybe good things really could come out of the bad. He wanted to believe that.

"You're thinking hard again," Mack teased.

"I know. I'm happy, and that's usually when everything goes completely to hell."

A shot rang out, echoing across the land outside the window. Brantley dropped to the floor, and Mack hunched down and hunted around for his phone. Brantley stayed still as Mack called in to the station.

"Get someone out here right away." Mack hung up and left the room, staying low.

Brantley finished pulling on his clothes. If something happened, the last thing he wanted was to have to explain to Mack's deputies why he was half-dressed when they arrived. "What happened?" Brantley called.

"I don't know. I don't see anything, and there doesn't seem to be any damage to the house."

Another shot rang out, this one farther away.

Mack returned to the bedroom as sirens sounded, getting closer. "I'm going out to meet my deputy. You stay here, just in case." He left.

Brantley sat on the edge of the bed, nervously waiting for news of whatever had happened. His heart pounded and blood raced through his ears. He was getting more than a little tired of all this.

When he returned, Mack said, "It was Erickson. He saw what he thought was a wolf and was trying to scare it off."

Brantley nodded. "I want all this to be over." He began to shake. He tried to get himself under control again and failed. Mack sat down and put his arms around him. "I'm sorry about this," Brantley said. "I thought I could handle it. But someone shooting a gun off

126

somewhere out back was enough for me to hit the floor. I hate being scared all the time, and you know what?" He turned to Mack. "I'd like to be able to go back to the diner to eat, but I honestly don't know if I can do that. Someone took a shot at me through a window. How much am I being watched? Sometimes I feel like I am. But am I really?"

"I wish I had answers for you. I know this is frightening, but we are going to catch this guy, and when I do, that will be the end of him. He's going to be put away for a very long time."

"You sound so sure. But this asshole broke into your house, and we haven't been able to catch him. What the hell is next? Am I going to be riding down the road in your truck and have a bullet come through the window, right into my head? I don't know, and it's starting to freak me out." Brantley stood and walked toward the bedroom door. "I'm trying to be strong. I really am. But I have to say that I don't know how much more of this I can take."

"I don't know what to say."

"I don't expect you to say anything. I know you're doing everything you can, and I appreciate that you listened to me. We've discovered some clues together. But maybe it would be best if I went back to New York for a while. I could visit some friends and get away from here. That would give you the chance to catch this guy, and then I could return." He turned to Mack.

Mack stayed seated. "If that's what you want to do, I can't stop you. But I don't want you to go. I like having you here." He stood and left the room.

Brantley picked up his bag and met Mack by the front door.

"Why do I get the feeling that once you go to New York, you won't come back?" Mack pulled open the door, and they stepped out.

Zeb was on his phone, standing near his cruiser. He hung up when he saw Mack. "There's another call I need to take. Shoplifting at the mercantile."

"Take it, and thanks for having my back," Mack told him.

Zeb took off, and Mack climbed into the truck.

Brantley locked the front door and got into the truck as well. He set his bag on his lap, hugging the thing to him. He could feel Mack pulling away, and he realized he'd probably made one of the biggest mistakes of his life, but he wasn't sure how to undo it and handle the fear that kept welling up inside.

CHAPTER 7

MACK'S STOMACH did flip-flops the entire drive back to the house. He called his dad on the way to make sure he was all right. When they got back to the house, he changed into his uniform and went in to the station. Once at his desk, he did his best to get into work mode and tried like hell to stop worrying about Brantley. At least he knew Brantley's truck wasn't ready yet, so unless he bought another vehicle, he was stuck in town for a few more days.

"Is Zeb back yet?" he asked Gloria from his office.

"No. He said he'll be back soon." She came to stand in his office doorway. "Who pissed in your Cheerios?"

"It's nothing."

"Yeah, sure." She rolled her eyes. "This wouldn't happen to have anything to do with the new guy in town who just happens to be staying at your place, would it? Is he hard to live with? I saw him the other day, and he's pretty cute. Do you think he's in the market for a girlfriend? My cousin Elise would be great for him, and we're all tired of the losers she tends to date, like Harley."

"I can safely say that Brantley isn't looking for a wife." He picked up some papers from his desk so he would have somewhere else to look and swallowed hard. This sort of conversation wasn't something he'd anticipated, but now that he thought about it, people were going to wonder about him and Brantley. He should have been prepared for this, but he found he wasn't… at least not as much as he'd like to have been. "Brantley is gay," he said flatly.

Gloria paused. "Okay. So no on my cousin." She seemed to be thinking. "Hmmm, my friend Donna has a son who is gay… maybe…."

"Gloria. Brantley doesn't need to be fixed up. He's already seeing someone." He realized this was a little fun.

"So soon? Who?"

"Gloria, who do you think? Me." He stared at her. And saw the light go on in her head.

"You?" Gloria's lower lip hung open for a whole second, then snapped closed. "Okay. So that's good, then. It's about time you found someone nice."

"You're not shocked?" Mack asked.

Gloria shrugged. "There are gay people everywhere. On television, in movies. What's the big deal? But I guess there are some folks who aren't going to be happy."

"I'm aware of that."

"What are you going to do?" Gloria asked. "The election is next year."

"Fight for my job," Mack said without thinking. "I'm a fine sheriff, and I've done a lot of good in this town. If people don't see that, then they deserve someone else, and I'll get a different job. There are plenty of things I can do."

"That a boy," Gloria said, turning away when the phone rang. She rushed back to the switchboard, and Mack got back to work, shaking his head in pleased surprise.

Zeb came into his office a half hour later and plopped himself into a chair. "God, I hate those calls."

"What happened?" Mack asked, setting the paperwork aside. He wasn't really reading it anyway.

"Peter Gunderson tried to take a video game. He didn't make it out the door because he kept looking around all the time. They called mainly to have me scare the kid."

"He's only eight," Mack said.

"Yeah, and he was in tears and could barely talk by the time I got there. He said he was sorry like half a million times, and when I asked why he took it, he said because his friend Barry had a copy and that he wanted to play with it, but Barry said he couldn't come over when he invited the other boys in their class to play. So he said he was going to take it and all he wanted to do was play it, and then he was going to bring it back, and that if he did that and said he was sorry, that it would be all right. He kept saying through his tears that he wasn't going to keep it. I talked to him, and it seems the other kids in his class pick on him a lot because he walks funny, and I think he wanted to have what they have."

"Oh God." Mack would have laughed if it wasn't so heartbreaking. "Did you call his mother?"

"I called the house, and Larry came out. He walked into the store under a head of steam like you wouldn't believe, but I calmed him down. I swear he was ready to punish Peter for the rest of his life. He was already promising never to do anything like that again, and when his dad did come inside, Peter tried to hide under the chair."

"Jesus. Do you think there's some abuse?" Mack asked. Stealing a game was one thing, but a kid in that much fear of his dad was something else.

"No. Larry was surprisingly gentle. I've seen him in his uniform, and he can be scary in fatigues, but once he got Peter out and away from the chair, he fell into his daddy's arms, crying and saying he was sorry."

"Are they going to press charges?"

"No. They got the game back, and it seems that Peter is going to be spending the next few Saturdays sweeping the store and sidewalk for them. And his video games have apparently been taken away for the foreseeable future." Zeb leaned forward. "And I said I'd make an appointment to go into the school to give a talk about bullying."

"That's a great idea." He could see the marks of bullying all over this incident. "If I'm able, I'll come with you." Mack waited to see if Zeb had anything more, but he got up to leave. "You did a really good job."

MACK WENT back to work, going over everything they'd found out, hoping like hell it presented the portrait of someone he knew. He always hated thinking that his neighbors and even his friends could be suspects, but he'd learned over the course of the job that not every suspect was an asshole or someone he didn't like. Sometimes he had to look objectively at neighbors and people he'd known for most of his life. That was the really difficult portion of his job. The advantage was that he knew everyone. So he continued looking at what he had. "This should be easier than this," he said out loud to no one in particular.

"Talking to yourself?" Gloria asked. "Things must be bad."

"Just a pain. I keep feeling like the answer is right in front of my face, and all I have to do is put the pieces together."

"Maybe it is," Gloria agreed and leaned over her desk. "The answers to most things are usually so simple that we look right past them." The phone rang and Gloria picked it up.

Mack rearranged some of his notes. "Holy shit," he mumbled under his breath. "Gloria," he yelled. "Where's Zeb?"

"I just sent him on a call," she told him.

"Where?" Mack grabbed his hat and hurried to her desk.

"The Roadhouse. They have some sort of disturbance."

Mack was already past her and out the door. He raced to his cruiser and took off out of the lot, heading out to the edge of town.

Even at this time of day, the Roadhouse was busy. Mack parked near the door and walked in to find plenty of yelling and some shoving. Zeb was trying to get it under control. "What the hell is going on?" Mack boomed over everyone. Instantly the place was as quiet as the cemetery. "That's enough." He turned to the bartender. "Who do you want removed?" He wasn't in any mood to sort out whatever stupid argument had started this. The bartender pointed to the usual troublemakers, and Zeb escorted them out just like that.

Mack followed them, the two men sputtering and fuming. "This is private property, and you have no right to be in there if the owners don't want you. I suggest you walk it off, because if either of you gets in a car, we'll throw both of you in jail." He didn't give them any quarter, and both men backed down and started walking toward town. Mack was pretty sure neither of them was particularly keen to call their wives to pick them up.

"I could have handled this," Zeb said.

"I know. I didn't come out here to step on your toes. But you said that Peter's father picked him up."

"Yeah. Larry said that Chrissy was down with the flu."

"But why is he home? Denny Beltz called Julie and said that his guard deployment was extended by a week. So why wasn't Larry's? They're in the same unit."

"I don't know. Maybe they only needed Denny," Zeb said, but Mack wasn't buying it.

"Thanks." Mack took off and called Gloria at the station. "Gloria, I need Larry Gunderson's phone number and address," he said. He waited, and once he got the information, he went to the Gunderson home. Larry worked nights at the hospital, so Mack was fairly sure he'd be there.

Mack pulled into the drive of the small but extremely neat house just off Main Street. He put the car in park and wasn't surprised at all when the front door opened as he walked up.

"Has Peter done something else?" Larry asked, yawning, dressed in a T-shirt and sweatpants.

"No," Mack answered. "But I need to speak with you."

Larry stepped back, and Mack went inside.

"I understand that you're in the same National Guard unit as Denny Beltz." Mack sat on the edge of one of the living room chairs while Larry collapsed back on the sofa. He hated interrupting Larry's sleep, but this couldn't wait.

"Yeah. Our annual training was the past two weeks, but we were done on Sunday."

"The entire unit?" Mack asked as he pulled out his notebook and pen.

"Well, yeah. We were all dismissed, and when we left, Denny was getting ready to go, the same as the rest of us." Larry seemed confused.

"Thanks."

Larry yawned and stood when Mack did. "I'm sorry about Peter. He and I have had a long talk, and while it doesn't excuse what he did, his mother and I are now aware that he was being bullied. I have an appointment to talk to the principal and his teacher tomorrow. We'll get to the bottom of this."

"Excellent. I'm sorry I disturbed you." Mack headed for the door. "Do you have your commander's phone number?"

"Certainly." Larry rattled it off, and Mack wrote it in his notebook and then thanked Larry once again.

"Perfect. I'll let you get some rest. I appreciate the help." Mack left the house and got into his cruiser as his phone rang. He answered it through the car. "Yes, Gloria," he said, backing out of the drive.

"We just received a call from Andy Erickson. He was checking on his herd and saw someone around the old Richardson house. He thought it looked suspicious and called it in. I was able to contact Brantley Calderone and he was heading out there, but I thought I should tell you too. Ronnie is on his way out there as well."

Mack's stomach roiled. In his gut he knew this was bad. He made a turn and raced out toward Brantley's ranch, sirens screaming and lights blazing. He pulled in the drive, parking next to his dad's car. Ronnie pulled in right behind him. Flames shot from some of the windows, and it was obvious they were gaining strength. The house would soon be completely engulfed.

"We need to find Brantley," Mack said as glass broke and smoke billowed out of the back of the house. "Get the fire department out here now," he yelled to Ronnie as he raced to the front door. He leaped onto the front porch and kicked open the door. Clouds of smoke poured out of the opening, followed by a wave of heat. He waited a few seconds for the air to clear and then raced inside.

The living room was filled with smoke. Mack coughed and scanned around. The kitchen was already being consumed, flames snaking their way toward the source of air. Mack knew there was no time to waste and launched himself down the hallway, pushing open each door. He had to find Brantley. He knew he was here.

The bathroom was empty, and so was the second bedroom. The master bedroom door was locked, and Mack kicked it in as the smoke around him grew thicker and the roar of the fire filled his ears. They didn't have much time.

The room was dark, curtains pulled, but the air was clear for a few seconds, just long enough for Mack to see a figure on the bed. Mack raced around the bed, practically pulling the curtains down in his haste to open them. Brantley was there, arms and legs duct-taped together. Mack tried to rouse him, but Brantley didn't respond.

Mack lifted him into his arms and hurried back the way he'd come, but a wall of roaring flame met him after two steps. That way was blocked, so he raced back into the bedroom and slammed the door. They had seconds before the flames broke through. Mack put Brantley back on the bed and opened the window, then pushed the screen out, letting it fall to the ground. "I need help in here," he yelled, hoping like hell Ronnie heard him.

He heard sirens but time was running out. Mack touched the wall and found it hot, radiating heat into the room and telling him the fire raged on the other side. He turned back to the bed and lifted Brantley once again, grateful when he heard a groan.

"Mack?" Ronnie called.

"Thank God. Brantley's here. I'm going to pass him through the window." He was already lifting him feetfirst through the opening. Ronnie grabbed hold of him, and it seemed so did the firefighters. The bedroom door burst inward and collapsed as Mack climbed through the opening. Men helped him through and to the ground before they all hurried away from the burning building.

Emergency personnel had Brantley on the ground and were giving him oxygen. One of the EMTs, Audie, offered Mack a mask, but he waved it away and slowly breathed in the fresh air. "I'm fine," he snapped. A large crash signaled that the house was falling in on itself, and when Mack turned, the kitchen side was mostly gone, sparks and embers flying high into the air. Water was being poured onto the house to try to keep the embers down, but there was nothing to be done otherwise. Mack could see the house was a total loss and within minutes would be nothing but a pile of ash and rubble. But that was a hell of a lot less important than the fact that Brantley was lying on the ground and he wasn't moving.

"Brantley," he said as he made his way over to where the person who had come to mean so much to him lay nearly motionless. "Why isn't he waking up? The room was clear of smoke, and I got him out before it got too bad." Just barely, but he'd been able to act fast.

"We're trying to figure that out, Sheriff," Audie said. "You need to stay back so we can work." He'd known Audie for a number of years, but his concern for Brantley was overriding everything else.

"Bullshit," Mack said and walked around to the far side, knelt on the ground, and took Brantley's hand, stroking it gently. "You need to wake up for me," he said quietly, paying little attention to the others around him. He had come to the decision that he was who he was, and holding back wasn't going to do him any good regardless. "Brantley, sweetheart, you need to open those amazing blue eyes and look at me."

"He has a lump on his head, but I don't think that's why he isn't waking up," Audie said. "I think he was given something to knock him out." He turned to the others. "We're going to transport him now. There isn't much more we can do here."

Mack backed away and watched as they lifted Brantley up and into the ambulance. Mack wanted desperately to ride with him, but he had a job to do here, and as much as he hated staying behind, he had to let the professionals do their job. "Do you think he'll be all right?"

Audie closed the back door of the ambulance. "I don't know. He could have been given a lot of things. I'll make sure they know to call you personally." He patted Mack on the shoulder and then hurried to the driver's seat, and seconds later the ambulance pulled away with the siren blaring.

"Is there anything I can do?"

Mack turned. He hadn't heard Julie Beltz come up behind him.

"Sorry," she said.

"No. Thanks." This was one of those shit times when doing his duty overrode what he really and truly wanted. He would be useless at the hospital, and here he could hopefully nail down who had done this.

"Was this an accident?" Julie asked.

Mack opened his mouth to say no but paused. He knew it wasn't, but he couldn't speak about ongoing investigations. "We're going to find out." He excused himself to talk with Captain Randall. "Whoever started the fire used accelerants," Mack told him. "I could smell them when I was inside. I don't think it was the whole house, but it wouldn't have gone up so fast otherwise."

"So this is arson?"

Mack shook his head. "Attempted murder." He wasn't going to pull any punches. "We need to investigate together." He wasn't about to get into a pissing contest.

"No problem. We can use all the help we can get. Most of our men are volunteers, so a joint investigation will work. And since I'm the lead investigator…."

"Good. It started in the back, right over there, then worked its way to the main section of the house and the bedroom last, which I don't understand, because if he truly wanted to kill Brantley, why didn't he start the fire in the room he was in?"

"Well, if I had to guess, I'd say the perpetrator wasn't a firebug. Those guys know how flame behaves. So I suspect he put the victim in the bedroom and then left the house, spreading his gasoline and then throwing a match before he hurried away. If he didn't wet everything, that would give him some time to get away and maybe out of sight before the heat broke a window and smoke would clearly be seen."

That made sense to Mack.

"Do you know who did it? Or think you know?"

"I have a good idea" was all that Mack would divulge. He did his best not to look at Julie. For her sake, he hoped he was wrong, but the evidence was adding up. "Thank you for everything. I'm going to get out of your way until you have this out." Mack went to his car, turned on the engine so the interior wouldn't become a blast furnace, and made the call that could clinch everything.

"Is this Byron Masters?" Mack asked when his call was answered.

"Captain Masters, yes," he confirmed gruffly.

"I'm Sheriff Mackenzie Redford from Hartwick County, and I'm hoping you can confirm something for me."

"I don't know." He sounded wary.

"I'm conducting a murder investigation, and I have some questions. Larry Gunderson gave me your name."

"Larry is one of my best sergeants. What can I help you with?"

"His unit recently had their two weeks of training."

He heard the rustle of papers. "Yes. They completed the training last weekend."

"Was anyone in his unit asked to stay an extra week?" Mack asked, praying for a positive answer.

More papers rustled in the background. "No. That entire unit was dismissed and sent home. They're a great unit and work well together. There was no reason for any of them to stay."

Mack's heart leaped and then fell. This was both the break in the case he'd been looking for and a huge disappointment, especially as he watched Julie standing with the few neighbors who were congregating. "Thank you."

"Are you saying that one of these men could be your suspect?"

"I can't answer that at this time, but I will contact you if charges are brought," Mack said.

"Fair enough," Captain Masters said. "I'm glad I could help."

"Would it be possible to get a copy of any paperwork that documents that the entire unit was dismissed?" Mack gave the captain his fax number, as well as e-mail address, and Captain Masters said he'd send a roster. He thanked the captain for his help and ended the call. "Shit!" he said inside the car, trying not to look like he was unhappy. There were too many people around for him to show this kind of emotion.

Mack got out, wondering how in the hell he would ever prove that Denny Beltz had been at the scene of the crimes. He had the boot print, but Denny wasn't the only person in town with those boots, and there could be others from out of town. So far he'd proved that Denny had lied to his wife, but that wasn't necessarily a crime. Denny had military expertise—that was a given. So Denny met all of the criteria they'd developed of their suspect, but the evidence was circumstantial. Mack had to find something more concrete, but at least now he knew where to start looking.

He got out of the car and did his best to try not to look like part of his world hadn't just crashed in on him. Denny was an old friend, and Mack looked after his family when he was away. The whole situation really pissed him off.

His phone rang and he practically jumped. "Sheriff Redford."

"It's Audie. I can't say much, but Brantley regained consciousness just before we reached the hospital. Privacy laws prevent us from saying more, but I wanted to let you know that he was talking and asking where you were. He doesn't remember very much about what happened, but he seems lucid."

"Thank you." Part of the knot in Mack's gut unwound. At least it sounded like Brantley was going to be okay. "Are you still with him?"

"I can be."

"Tell him that I'll be there just as soon as I can."

"I will," Audie agreed, and Mack thanked him and hung up.

The house was still too hot to enter, so Mack instructed Ronnie to stay on-site and not to allow anyone to enter the wreckage until he returned. Mack ran back to his car and pulled out, calling his dad as he raced home.

"Mack," Lew said as he answered the phone.

"Are you okay?" Mack asked in a rush.

"Yes, I'm fine."

"Call someone and get them to sit with you. I don't want you alone. Hell, get half your friends and tell them you're having a party. Eat everything in the house, just get people over there."

"You know something."

"Yeah, and don't let anyone under fifty in the house. I have a suspect, and I can't say who it is, but do not stay alone."

"Okay. I'll make calls."

"You have five minutes," Mack said and hung up. He continued toward town, hands shaking until his dad called back to ask if Gordy across the street was clear. Mack told him that was fine, and apparently Gordy was on his way to sit with him until other friends could come over. "Keep your eyes open, Dad, and call in if you see anything suspicious." He continued to the station, went to his desk, and sat looking at all the things he had.

The one thing he didn't want to do at the moment was to serve a warrant on Julie. He had the probable cause to search the house, but that would be traumatic for them, and what if he was wrong? And he wondered if Denny would bolt if he got word of it, and that particular bit of news was bound to get around town in record time.

He looked up at a knock on the doorframe.

"Mack," Zeb said. "I heard about what happened. When you see Brantley, tell him I'm sorry about his house and that I hope he's doing better."

"I will," Mack said. "Come in here and close the door." He waited for Zeb to comply and then went over what he had. "I think I know who's behind all this."

Zeb's eyes widened. "That's great."

"No, it's not. It's Denny Beltz."

"No way!" Zeb leaped to his feet. "He has…."

"I know. The thing is, he has the kind of boot we are looking for, military experience, and he wasn't at training for an extra week. No one from his unit was asked to stay longer. Brantley and I found gold on the ranch property he bought. So I think that's why Denny has been trying to run Brantley off. The problem is that I can't tie him directly to the crimes. It's all circumstantial. I knew there was something I was missing."

"What can I do?"

"We need to go over everything we have again."

"We checked the casings we recovered for prints but found none," Zeb said.

"I want you to look at those boot photographs again. Enlarge them, or get Ronnie to help if you need it, to see if there is anything special about them. Maybe we can match them to a specific boot." He knew that would only help if they could recover the pair of boots. He was grasping at straws. Mack groaned. "I'm going to have to bite the bullet and have a talk with Julie. It's going to hurt like hell, but I have to see what I can find out."

"Are you sure she'll cooperate?"

"I can get a warrant if I have to." He hoped that wouldn't be necessary. This whole thing was turning out to be a minefield. But he'd navigated them before, and he'd do it again. "I need to go see Brantley as well."

"You do what you have to, and I'll review everything and go over all the evidence again. There could be something when seen through fresh eyes."

Mack nodded. God, he hoped he was right. If he wasn't, he was going to create a great deal of pain for dear friends. He reluctantly stood, still running through everything that he'd gathered. He knew he needed to pay Julie a visit, but he put that off. "I'm going to go check on Brantley." He needed to see him and know he was okay. Thinking clearly wasn't happening at the moment. "If you come up with anything, call me right away."

"I will, Sheriff."

"We should also put out an APB on Denny's truck."

"I'll do that right away," Zeb said.

"And it goes without saying to keep all this to yourself. I don't want the rumor mill to pick up on all this."

Zeb got up, and Mack followed him out of the office. Zeb went right to his desk, and Mack left the station and went to his cruiser. He intended to go from the hospital to Julie's, and that needed to be an official visit.

The ride to the small county hospital took less than five minutes, and he parked as close as he could to the door, then strode inside and up to the desk.

An older woman looked up from her computer, and her eyes widened and she licked her lips. "Can I help you?"

"Brantley Calderone's room, please."

She typed. "He's in room 212. Is he in trouble?"

Mack thanked her, ignoring the question, and headed down the hall. He'd been here plenty of times and knew where he was going. People got out of his way, and normally he'd smile and greet them, but the closer he got to Brantley, the faster he moved and the harder his chest pounded. He paused outside the room and then stepped into the doorway.

Brantley lay on the bed, his eyes closed. A monitor next to his bed displayed his pulse and heart rate, as well as the last blood-pressure reading. There might have been other things displayed, but Mack paid them little attention and focused on the man in the bed.

"Mack," Brantley said in a groggy voice.

"I'm here. How are you feeling?" He sat down next to him and gently took Brantley's hand.

"Like I've been run over by a steamroller. I was injected with something, I think. I don't know what, and then that was it."

"Did you see who it was?" That could be the hard proof he needed.

"No. It was from behind, and I remember being dragged down the hall as I passed out. The man from the ambulance said you saved me and got me out of the house."

"Yeah. Whoever drugged you set it on fire, but I got there first and got you out the window." Mack's hand shook. "You scared me half to death. I didn't know if you were going to make it, and…." He swallowed hard. It was difficult talking about his feelings, but damn it, he'd nearly lost Brantley, so this was not the time to hold back. "I was scared that I'd never get to look in your eyes or be able to tell you that you've come to mean the world to me. I wanted to stay with you and be here when you woke up."

"You had a job to do."

"I did, and I think I might know who is behind all this, but I can't prove it yet." Mack got his mind back on what was important. "Seeing you on the ground, not waking up, made me realize just how much I love you and that if I didn't get off my ass and say something to you, I was going to regret it." He lightly stroked the back of Brantley's hand.

"I know how you feel. I was passing out, and all I could think of was you and how I might not get to see you again." Brantley turned his head toward him on the pillow. "You think you know who it is?"

"Yeah. But we don't have to talk about that now."

"I want to know."

Mack knew he shouldn't say anything, but Brantley had been working pretty closely on this case. Still he hesitated before answering. "I think it was Denny Beltz. Julie said he'd called to say that he had been required to stay another week in Reserves, but he wasn't. He lied to her, and I got the proof from his captain today. He also has the training to take the shots, and he owns a pair of the boots that made the print. He had the opportunity and means because no one was looking for him."

"But why?" Brantley asked. "For him to go to all this trouble, there has to be more to it. Does he need money? Can you place him at any of the scenes?"

"I don't know about the money, but I need to find that proof. Ronnie is great with electronics, and he's going to look at the boot print image to see if there is anything unique about it. Denny covered his tracks so well that while I have circumstantial evidence, I don't have hard proof, and that is really pissing me off." Mack stood and walked to the end of the bed. "He's tried to hurt you so many times, and I almost lost you because of him. I'm ready to tear him apart—job, along with everything else, be damned."

"What you need to do is find him. How long have you known him?"

"Fifteen years. Since we were kids."

"Then ask yourself where he'd go and see if you don't get lucky. People return to places they're familiar with and where they feel safe. If he's been watching us and gone to these lengths, he's not going to give up now. He knows I have to be scared shitless. So you might put the word out through the grapevine that I've decided to leave town and that I'm going to put the ranch up for sale again and be done with it. Use that as bait and see if it doesn't shake some of the leaves off the trees. Once I get out of here, we can figure out how we make that look good. Then we can see who comes forward."

"Give them what they want. You're brilliant."

"I like to think so," Brantley said, smiling for the first time.

Mack returned it. "How do we get them to act quickly?"

Brantley closed his eyes, and Mack sat quietly, wondering if Brantley had fallen asleep, but then Brantley said, "I think we need to say that you heard that one of my friends from New York was interested in the property. Make it time sensitive, so they have to act quickly. I bet you know just the right person to tell and get the word going."

"I do," Mack said. Gloria would be perfect, and so would Marlene, especially if he could arrange for them to overhear what he wanted them to pass on. "Brantley, what about you?" He was tired of talking about the case. "How long will you be here?"

"They want to keep me overnight to make sure that whatever I was given is completely out of my system," Brantley said, sounding hoarse, and Mack got his cup of water from the tray and held the straw to his lips. After Brantley took a sip, he said, "They said I should be fine but want to be sure. The only question I have is how am I going to make it seem like I've left town without actually leaving town?" Brantley put the straw to his lips and drank again.

"We could check with the garage to see if your truck is fixed. You could pick it up, and I'd have one of the deputies drive it out of town. Then you'd stay at the house and keep out of sight."

Brantley closed his eyes once again. "Maybe this is just too complicated to pull off."

"Are you saying that you want to leave for real?" Mack asked with a sinking feeling in his gut.

"Honestly, I think I'm saying that you need to try to solve the case so we don't have to go through all this crap." Brantley opened his eyes and slowly repositioned himself. "Maybe my first idea about playing like I'm leaving town is over the top. I'm not thinking too clearly, and I don't think I want to be scared away or to let people think I can be. After we catch this guy, I want to be able to live here and have friends here. What will they think if I appear to run?"

Mack didn't have an answer for him. More than anything he wanted Brantley safe and secure. "All right." He leaned over the bed. "I have a murderer to catch, and I'm going to see what I can do."

"I wish I could go with you."

"You stay here and be safe." He kissed Brantley on the lips, savoring his sweetness before pulling away. "I'd feel so much better if I could take you with me. I could make sure you were safe."

"The only guarantee is if you catch this guy and put him away. Then I'll be safe, and we can begin living a life." Brantley held out his hand, and Mack took it, gently holding Brantley's fingers.

"I'll see you as soon as I can." Mack let his hand slip from Brantley's and then turned to leave the room. He did peer back to take one last look before heading to the nurse's station. He explained that Mr. Calderone was to have no visitors and that he would let the desk know downstairs. Within a few minutes he was face-to-face with a hospital administrator.

"It's for his safety and that of your staff."

"No problem, Sheriff. We'll make sure that he's removed from our visitor system so anyone who checks won't be given his room number."

"Thank you," Mack said, shaking his hand, and then hurried toward the exit. There were times when he wished he had more personnel, but his budget was severely limited and his deputies were all assisting him. Brantley was right: the sooner Mack apprehended Denny, the sooner this would all be over.

Mack left the hospital and hurried to his cruiser, then took off out of the parking lot and out toward Julie's.

"Sheriff Mack," Nathan called as soon as he got out of the car.

"Hi, Nathan," Mack said as gently as he could. "Is your mom here?"

He pointed and then ran toward the barn. "Mommy, Sheriff Mack is here," he yelled as he ran.

Mack smiled and walked behind him, finding Julie feeding the horses.

"Mack, it's good to see you. It was a real shame about what happened to Brantley's house. Is he all right?"

145

"Yes. He's very shaken up and more than a little scared, but I guess that's to be expected after all that's happened." Mack stepped a little closer and lowered his voice. "Is there someplace we can talk? I don't want to frighten Nathan."

Julie dropped the hay she'd been carrying into the nearest manger. "Of course," she said warily. "Is something wrong?"

"I'm not sure, and I hope you can help me find out." He stepped away, and Julie took Nathan's hand.

"Why don't you come with me? You can watch *Dora* for a little while." She led an excited and chattering Nathan across to the house and got him settled on the sofa in front of the television. "We'll be on the front porch if you need us," she said once he was settled and watching a DVD. He was completely engrossed within a few seconds, and Mack followed Julie out to the porch.

Julie sat in one of the wicker chairs, and Mack leaned against the railing. He'd practiced what he wanted to say and how he wanted to start this conversation on the way over, but those words flew out of his mind.

"Julie, can I ask if things have been good between you and Denny?"

She shrugged. "We have our ups and downs. Things have been more down than up these past few months. I'm hoping that when he gets home, the weeks apart will have been good for me, at least. We both needed a chance to breathe." She turned to check inside the house. "I haven't told Nathan about our problems."

"What kind of issues?" Mack asked as carefully as he could and tried to sound less like a cop and more like a concerned friend even though he was in uniform.

Julie blew air through her lips in what Mack interpreted as exasperation. "The ranch hasn't been doing very well. He wants us to cut our losses, and I'm trying to fight to keep what my family and I have built here. It's been the source of a number of arguments."

Mack saw the fire in her eyes. It was the kind that it took to keep a place like hers going. Ranches existed on cattle, horses, hard work, and piles of determination and grit. Mack knew that, and he knew Julie had it in spades.

"Have you heard from Denny in the last few days?"

"He called to talk to Nathan the other day. I talked to him for a few minutes. He said he's been very busy but should be home this weekend. He said he was training some new people and that it was going very well."

Mack sighed and knew he had to come clean. He wished like hell he didn't have to be the one giving her the bad news. "Julie, you know I'm here in uniform and it isn't just a social call. I talked to Larry Gunderson, and he wasn't asked to stay. That got me curious, so I called Denny's commanding officer. He said that no one from Denny's unit was asked to stay an extra week."

Julie blinked at him, staring as though she was trying to comprehend what he had just told her. "So he isn't at Reserves?"

"No. And I'm trying to determine his whereabouts. We found boot prints at my house after it was broken into that match a brand of boot that Denny has, and it seems that the mercantile hasn't sold many pairs. There is also the shot that was taken through the diner window and the one taken to Brantley's front porch. That one in particular took some skill."

"So you're accusing Denny?" she asked with a bite in her voice.

"No. But he did lie about where he was, and I need to know where he's been. I was hoping it would be all right for me to take a look at his guns and if you could tell me if any are missing."

Julie sat still. "My first instinct is to tell you to fuck the hell off. But I've known you for years, and I know you'd never do this unless you didn't have a good reason." She slowly stood and walked to the door. "I refuse to believe that Denny could do anything like tie someone up and leave them in a burning house to die or try to shoot someone, even that husband-stealing bitch, Renae." She stopped with her hand on the door. "God, you don't think Denny was having an affair with her, do you?" She trembled and her shoulders slumped forward.

"What I'm hoping I can prove is that it wasn't him and then figure out where he was so that I can remove him from my list. And I have no evidence that he was having an affair." In fact, Renae's appointment book had yielded no information whatsoever about the men she'd been seeing. That part of the case had been a dead end, and maybe for the town itself that was a good thing. Renae might have been a cougar on the prowl, but she didn't have to rip apart half the marriages in town.

"Okay," Julie said, her voice turned defeated. "Come on. I'll show you where we keep the guns." Julie opened the door, and Mack followed her inside.

Nathan sat on the sofa, legs curled up, enthralled in the television. Mack stopped, watching him, wondering about the impact on this innocent, adorable child if what he suspected was true. There were times when his job completely sucked. Nathan looked from the television to them and then went right back to his show. Mack continued on to the office.

Julie had opened the gun safe. "There's one missing," she said with remarkable calmness, and Mack wondered if she was going into a sort of shock.

"What kind is it?"

"A Browning 300 Win Mag. Denny has used it a few times for hunting elk," Julie answered, and fuck if that didn't match the shells and bullets they'd recovered. Mack did his best to keep that information off his face. He didn't need to worry Julie unnecessarily, although the case against her husband was becoming tighter and tighter. "I have the paperwork on it here somewhere." Julie opened one of the file drawers and pulled out a file folder, found what she wanted, and handed him the brochure with the receipt attached.

"Thank you," Mack said, taking the paperwork as though it was red hot. This was the link he was looking for, and now he needed to find Denny and the gun. "Do you mind if I look around? I'm not going to dig through things." He wanted to make this as easy as possible.

"Just do what you need to. I'm going to sit with Nathan." She turned away and left him alone in the office.

Mack looked around the room, determined to keep his promise. He left the office and went to the back mudroom. The floor under the blue awning-stripe upholstered bench seat was a jumble of kid and adult shoes. Some were obviously Denny's, but his boots weren't among them. He went from room to room, methodically searching for the boots. The house was meticulously clean, with very little dust under the beds and definitely no boots. The closets were the same. Mack didn't want to push things with Julie since he was here on her goodwill.

Mack joined her in the living room. "Thank you."

"Nothing?" she asked, gathering Nathan a little closer.

"No. I appreciate the help. Thank you." Mack shared a smile with Nathan and then left the house, going back to his squad car. He pulled away and followed his nose. He had to find Denny, and that meant checking some of the out-of-the-way places he knew Denny frequented. The first of which was a now-abandoned junkyard outside of town. He drove that way, making the turns until the pile of car hulks showed on the horizon. A number of people had petitioned the county to clean up the place, but there was no money, so the skeletons of once stylish vehicles decayed more and more each year. It had been abandoned when he was in school, so when he pulled to a stop and got out, the yard was even more overgrown and the cars less identifiable.

Rust prevailed as he wandered slowly through the rows, the wind dancing and whistling around, churning up little clouds of dust. Other than that and the occasional animal scurrying, there was no sound other than the scuff of his own feet. Mack kept his hand on his gun, going row to row, looking for some sign that someone had been there recently, but the ground was surprisingly undisturbed. If someone had been living out here, there would be some sort of coming and going unless Denny had gone to great lengths to hide his tracks, and given what he'd done, Mack thought that was a possibility. Still, as he made his way around, he became more and more convinced that there was no one here now.

Mack sighed and walked back to his car. He got in and pulled away.

"Sheriff." Gloria's voice boomed through the radio. "We got a call on the Beltz APB," she said, and Mack acknowledged the message and cringed before calling the station through his phone. There were too many people in the county with police band radios. "Sheriff, I'm sending you to Ronnie." The phone beeped.

"Ronnie, what do we have?"

"His truck was spotted thirty miles north of here, heading this way. We got lucky as shit. They thought he seemed to be heading back toward us on Taylor highway."

"I'm heading that way now. Have Zeb meet me along the way. I went to the Beltz ranch and a 300 Win Mag seems to be missing."

Ronnie whistled. "If we recover it, I can test fire and match the bullets. I was able to take detailed photographs of those we recovered for comparison."

"Okay. Get Zeb out here right away. We need to get Denny into custody." Mack hung up and listened to the radio calls. He drove cautiously until Zeb caught up with him, and then both of them sped up as fast as safety allowed.

After ten minutes, Mack pulled off to the side of the road, turned around, and waited. He got on the radio and said to Zeb, "Go on up a few miles, right at the county line, and wait. Don't pull out or signal, just let me know when he's on the way. Once he's out of sight, follow at a safe distance as backup. I'll pull him over and wait to approach until you arrive."

"Got it," Zeb said and continued down the road.

Mack settled in, watching in his rearview mirror.

Five minutes later, Zeb radioed that Denny's truck had just passed him. "Couldn't see the driver," he added, and Mack acknowledged the call.

Mack waited. It should have taken just a few minutes for Denny to reach him, but no truck appeared. "Are you sure it was him?"

"Yes. I'm following. Should be a mile behind…. Sheriff, you need to get back here."

Mack pulled onto the country highway, turned on his lights and siren, and raced. He saw Zeb's car and slowed, pulling off the road.

He got out, and Zeb pointed to where Denny's truck had gone off the road, down a ravine, and was resting on its roof. Zeb took off with Mack right behind him.

The truck had rolled more than once, one of the back wheels spinning freely. The other back tire seemed to have blown out and was shredded.

"Call the fire department and an ambulance," Mack instructed as he knelt on the ground to peer inside. Denny Beltz hung in his seat by the belt. "Denny, can you hear me?" Mack asked, but Denny didn't move or answer. He raced to the other side of the truck, the scent of gasoline burning his nose. He ignored it, knowing there was no time to lose, and reached inside the now nonexistent window. Denny was alive, he could tell from the pulse.

"They're on their way," Zeb called.

"We need to get this door open," Mack called. He was able to unlatch the door, and it opened a few inches. Zeb joined him and added his strength. The metal protested and then slowly the door opened enough that Mack could reach inside to unhook Denny's seat belt and drag him from the truck as the gasoline fumes continued to build. His eyes watered, but together with Zeb, they were able to get Denny away from the truck and up to the side of the road.

Zeb got a blanket from his car and laid it on the ground, and Mack settled Denny on it while they waited for help. "I hope we didn't hurt him worse," Zeb said.

"That truck can go up at any time. The fuel tank is leaking and...." A sizzle caught his attention, followed by flames that quickly engulfed the entire truck. The heat was intense enough that he turned away and fell to the ground. Thankfully the heat lasted just a few seconds and then dissipated. A cloud of black smoke rose high into the air. He didn't want to move Denny again, but the breeze was unpredictable, so he and Zeb carefully dragged Denny on the blanket to a safer spot.

"Flag down the ambulance and fire department when they get close. This area is dry enough that if this fire isn't brought under control quickly, it's going to spread, and then we'll have a grass fire to contend with."

Zeb hurried away, and Mack once again checked for Denny's pulse. It was slow and he was breathing, but not healthily, by any means. Mack stayed close and listened for sirens, which took another ten minutes. When the ambulance and fire truck arrived, they pulled to a stop and got right to it. Mack let the EMTs work on Denny and stayed out of the way of the firefighters while they brought the burning truck under control. Mostly they doused the perimeter to let the truck burn out.

"What happened?" Captain Randall asked once he and Mack were able to talk.

"I think he had a blowout and lost control of the truck. The one tire was shredded, but it's hard to say, and most of the evidence I'd need to know for sure went up in flames." One of the cardinal rules of crime scene investigation was that human life came first, and getting Denny out of the truck and away from danger was worth more than being able to get a look at what had remained of the tire, which was now gone.

"How did you get out here so fast?"

"We were looking for him. He's a suspect in an investigation," Mack explained, keeping his answer vague. The truck was already burning down, the fire having consumed most of what there was to burn.

"That's going to be hot for a while."

"Zeb will establish a perimeter as soon as you and your men are done." There was nothing else he could do. The fire had to be contained so it would burn out. He couldn't have a large portion of the county blazing with an uncontrolled grass fire. Public safety also took precedence.

He let Captain Randall do his job and checked in with the EMTs, who were ready to transport Denny to the hospital. "He is a suspect," Mack said. "I'll have someone meet you at the hospital." Mack called Ronnie from his car and explained what he needed.

This entire case was stressing his department to the limit, but he was determined to see it through. Once he was done with his call, Mack returned to the scene as the ambulance pulled out, heading toward town with blaring sirens.

"At least we got him," Zeb said.

"Yeah, but did you happen to notice anything strange?" Mack asked.

"Like what?"

"His boots?" Mack answered. "They weren't the ones we are looking for. The ones he had on are completely different. The interior of the truck cab was clear. There wasn't anything lying inside."

"I don't understand."

"Exactly. There wasn't a gun or anything like that."

"It could have been in the back."

"That's a possibility. The gun we're looking for costs nearly a thousand dollars new. Granted, Denny's gun is probably older, but with something like that, you aren't going to throw it in the bed of the truck where it can roll around and slide back and forth. It's going to be in a case inside where it can be protected."

"It could have been behind the seat," Zeb suggested, and Mack shook his head.

"The back of the seat was sprung. If it had been there, it would have fallen out. It didn't." Mack rolled the facts around in his mind.

"What do you think that means?"

"That as soon as it's safe, we need to check every inch of this area. If it was in the back, then it would have been thrown out when the truck rolled, and we need to find it. We have to know what he had with him."

"Sheriff, what are you thinking?" Zeb asked.

"Nothing in particular. We just need to search this scene with a fine-tooth comb." That wasn't the whole truth, but he had a feeling in his gut that wasn't going away. It felt a lot like excitement, and he wanted to make sure that if there was any evidence to be found, they located it as soon as possible.

"But he ran off the road," Zeb said.

"Did he? Do we know that for sure? Until we prove otherwise, this is a crime scene, and we'll treat it as such. So we're going to need gloves, of course. Also, I'm going to need someone to remain here to control the scene. It's going to be many hours before the truck is cool enough for us to work—" Mack was interrupted by a hiss of steam as the fire department poured water onto what was left of the truck. That doused the last of the flames, but it wouldn't do much to cool the truck's body, and the tanker only carried so much water.

"We're going to remain here until we're sure there won't be a flare-up," Captain Randall said.

"There's a creek with water in it a mile up the road. You can probably pump some more water if you wanted," Zeb said, and Mack figured Zeb would have brought the water himself by the bucketful if it meant he wouldn't have to sit out here all night to wait for the truck to cool.

"Great." Captain Randall instructed the tanker to head up the road for water. "We can dump another tank on it, and that will ensure that it's out permanently."

"Good," Mack said and stepped away. He made a call to his dad, who was apparently in the middle of some sort of game that he thought was hilarious.

"We have to get us a copy of this Cards Against Humanity. It's a hoot. Gordy called some of his friends, and we're having a game party." The laughter in the background told him all he needed to know. "They brought that game, and believe it or not, I'm winning. It's hysterical."

"Okay. I'm going to be out for a while yet, and I don't want you to be alone."

"Gordy and his friends will be here for a while I think…. Oh, and we're out of beer."

Mack stifled a groan. It was a small price to pay. "Just have fun and I'll call again as soon as I can." He hung up and shook his head. He was happy his dad was enjoying himself and safe. That was what mattered. Hell, his father never ceased to surprise him, and Mack hoped that never changed. He was truly blessed with an outstanding dad who had done an amazing job as both father and mother. He really couldn't ask for more.

Once he hung up, Mack called the hospital and asked for Brantley's room.

"Hello," Brantley answered softly.

"Did I wake you?" Mack asked.

"Kind of, but I'm glad you called. It's been so quiet here. The doctor stopped in just after you left, and they're running a few more tests to ensure that the sedative I was given is all gone."

Mack made a note to see the doctor in order to get a report of what they found. This case had so many moving pieces right now that he felt like he was unwinding a Gordian knot in order to get at the truth. "Did he say when he expected you to be able to come home?"

"Tomorrow morning," Brantley answered.

"Good. You get some rest, and I'll be over to see you as soon as I can. I have a crime scene I need to investigate, and I'm hoping this will tell the tale about exactly what's going on." He sure as hell hoped so, because in order for everyone important in his life to be safe, he needed to solve this case.

CHAPTER 8

AFTER HE hung up with Mack, Brantley spent the next hour or so dozing, and then he was wide awake. Whatever he'd been given seemed to have worn off, because after dinner he turned on the television and watched whatever crap he could find. He was getting really bored and was thrilled when his nurse came in.

"How are you feeling?" she asked cheerily.

"Bored out of my skull, wide awake, and I feel like I want to get up and do something, anything."

"No sleepiness or hazy thinking?"

"Nope. My mind is clear, and the stuff on television is—" He paused midcomplaint. There was nothing she could do about it. He needed to make the best of where he was until he could go back to Mack's.

"You certainly seem better," the nurse said, checking the machine. "Everything looks good here too. Rest is the best thing for you now."

"I know, but I'm not tired at all. I've slept most of the day, and I don't think I can any longer," Brantley told her as she went about fluffing his pillow.

"Just rest, and after the doctor comes in tomorrow morning, you should be able to go home." She placed the call button near his hand. "Be sure to call if you need anything." She smiled at him and left the room.

Brantley stared at the screen, watching just to pass the time.

Hours later he wondered if Mack was going to make it in time to see him. It was after nine when Mack walked into his room, looking like hell and smelling of smoke. "What happened?"

Mack sat in the chair next to his bed. "I've had a rough night. We got a report that Denny Beltz's truck was seen on its way toward town. I went out to meet it, and before I could stop him, he ran off the road. His truck flipped. Zeb and I got him out before the truck burst into flames."

"Is he alive?" Brantley asked.

"Yes. As of right now, he's here in the hospital. He had emergency surgery because the accident caused internal damage, and he hasn't woken yet."

"Did you find what you were looking for?"

"That's why I'm so late. He wasn't wearing the boots, and they weren't in the cab of the truck. Neither was the gun. We looked everywhere for them because they might have been thrown from the truck when it flipped. We found nothing." He took a deep breath and sat back in the chair, clearly exhausted. "Once we got the truck processed and then flipped over, they weren't under it either. That section was largely protected from the flames, and the paint was mostly intact in the bed, so if they'd been stowed there, they'd still be there, but they weren't. We did find a tent and some camping equipment. Fishing poles, but no gun."

"So no boots and no gun—that means he could have stashed them somewhere else."

"Why would he do that? He doesn't know about the print. No one does. So why would he dump his boots?" Mack shook his head. "He was wearing an old pair of boots. We gathered everything we found, and tomorrow I'll see what I can put together."

"How did you get so dirty?"

"We sifted out the contents of the cab to see if we could find anything. I have it all locked up in evidence and need to evaluate it in the morning."

"Do you have a theory about what all this means?"

"I have dozens of them, but I'm too tired to think clearly. I'm hoping Denny can tell us something once he wakes up. It certainly looks like he's been camping, and I'd really like to know where he's been."

"Like in the woods near my ranch so he could watch me?" Brantley asked, the anger he'd held at bay rising in his voice. "I want you to catch this asshole and nail him to the wall. He burned down my house and tried to kill me more than once." He clenched his fists.

"Relax. I'm getting really close to the end of this. I can feel it now. When I can think clearly, we're going to review everything and piece together the entire picture of exactly what's happening. And Lord knows, Denny isn't going anywhere." Mack looked thirsty, and Brantley passed the glass of water from his tray to Mack. "Thank you."

"Welcome," Brantley answered, the way he'd heard some of the locals do. "You really think you got him?"

"Yeah. There are still outstanding questions, but I do." Mack yawned. "With what his wife told me, they've been having troubles and the ranch isn't doing well. So I suspect he wanted your place so he could go for the gold that was there and try to stave off foreclosure. With you gone, the place was certain to sell cheaply, being the scene of a murder and all." He kept his voice low.

"Do you think he had a thing with Renae? Is that why he went after her? I mean, he could have killed me with that shot through the diner window, but didn't, and I don't think that was some accident. He didn't want to kill me, only put the fear of God in me so I'd run." Brantley thought for a while. "You know, it's very possible that he ditched the boots and gun long before he decided to come back toward town."

"There are still too many unanswered questions for my liking. I'm hoping that Denny will open up once he knows I have him dead to rights, and then I can tie this case up in a nice little bow and be done with it. The town will be happy and feel safe once again, and by solving the murder, I hope most people will be willing to overlook the whole gay thing at election time."

"I'll feel so much better once this is wrapped up, and then I can figure out what I'm going to do about a house. I'd like to rebuild, I think. Maybe a place with a little city elegance in the country." Brantley chuckled. "I've had lots of time to think while I was lying here." He'd also thought how lonely he would be once Mack didn't need to keep him close anymore and he stopped living in Mack's guest room. That was going to be difficult.

"I'm sure you could build whatever you wanted. But there's no hurry. You've got a place to stay as long as you need it." Mack sighed and then leaned closer to his bed. "You need to make the decisions that are right for you, and you're going to need some time to work things out. Hell, I'm sort of hoping you have a tough time deciding." He smiled, and Brantley closed his eyes and Mack brought his lips to his.

Brantley would never get used to how good that felt and tasted, or how heat never failed to sizzle up his spine just from that simple touch. He loved it and slowly wound one arm around Mack's neck. The click of steps in the hallway receded, as did the general soft buzz of conversation from the nurses' station, along with the overlapping drone of patient televisions—all of it falling away as he basked in the warm glow of Mack's eyes and the melting heat from his lips. That was all he needed to feel better, and his dick was now as wide awake as the rest of him. God, he wanted Mack so badly. Time alone to think had allowed his mind to wander over many things, including how nice it would be for Mack to pummel his lips, sink his thick cock between his cheeks, filling him and letting him know that everything was going to be all right, just because Mack was there.

Mack broke the kiss when his phone rang. He groaned, answered it, and spoke softly before hanging up. From the stormy yet sad expression, the news wasn't good. "It's going to be a while, if at all, before Denny wakes up." Mack put his phone away.

"I know you're tired. Go on and go home. Try to get some rest."

"I will. Call me when they let you out of here, and I'll come get you and take you to the house where I can look after you." The relief in Mack's voice was palpable. "If he doesn't wake, I may never get the answers I'm looking for, but there isn't a doubt in my mind that he's the one behind this. And either way, it's over. I'm going to file all my reports and paperwork so I can get a warrant, and that should be that."

Brantley nodded, and when Mack kissed him again, it took all Brantley's self-control not to pull him down on the bed. "That should give you something to look forward to."

Mack brought his lips to Brantley's ear, hot breath sending a shock through him. "When I get you home, I intend to celebrate the end of this case well into the night. Maybe I'll give Dad ear plugs so I can make you scream when I eat out that pretty ass of yours before fucking you hard until you can't remember your own damn name."

Brantley's cock throbbed, and he had the urge to palm it, but touching himself in a situation like this was not the best idea. "I thought I was the only one with time on his hands."

"With you, it doesn't take much. I'm on the edge just thinking about you." Mack sucked on his ear, and then his lips slipped away. He stood over the bed, looking, and Brantley watched him in return, wondering what was going through his mind at that moment. "Get some rest, sweetheart, and I'll pick you up in the morning."

"You too. This is over now, and you can get some sleep." Brantley took Mack's hand. "I'll never forget how you took care of me when I needed it."

"Hey. It was a two-way street." Mack squeezed Brantley's fingers. "I really think we make a good team."

Brantley kept expecting Mack to turn to leave, but he stayed and stayed. They didn't talk. Mack held his hand and turned slightly toward the door more than once, but he stayed where he was until Brantley's eyelids began feeling heavy. Then Mack kissed him once again and left the room.

Brantley slept soundly, no longer having to keep one ear out for something to go horribly and dangerously wrong. Even so, his dreams were filled with replays of him finding Renae and the shooting. The shot kept ringing in his ears. In his dream he could never see the shooter, but he always got so close. His dreams changed as the night progressed. First it was him, and then Lew was the target, then it was him again, along with Mack. Soon his mind was conjuring up images of a shooting gallery with all of them as targets, moving to someone else's movements.

Brantley woke with a start, his eyelids flying open.

"It's all right," the nurse said from next to his bed.

"What time is it?" Brantley asked, rubbing his eyes.

"Just after six. I'll be out of here in a few minutes, and you can go back to sleep."

"What's your name?" Brantley asked.

"Nadine." She smiled softly. He hadn't heard that name in a very long time. It was unusual, and he said so. "I was named after my grandmother. I need to take a little blood from you so we can do one more set of tests before we send you home." She did what she needed and then straightened his bedding and got him comfortable before leaving the room.

Brantley closed his eyes and tried to go back to sleep. He was a little too excited to really fall deeply to sleep. When he woke an hour or so later, there was a visitor in his room.

"Morning, Julie," Brantley said.

"I heard you were in here," she told him, moving closer to the bed. "I guess you were very lucky to have gotten out of the house." She didn't smile, and something in her eyes sent a chill up his spine.

"Are you here to visit Denny?"

"Eventually." Her gaze didn't turn away from him, and Brantley squirmed under its intensity. She'd always seemed so confident when he'd visited her, but now she looked harried and one hand flicked against her thigh every few seconds. "I wanted to see that you were all right." Each time she said something, the air grew just a little colder. There was something very off. Of course, finding out your husband was a murderer was enough to make anyone a little scattered.

"I'm sorry about everything. This all has to be so hard for you. If there's anything I can do…."

Julie's misery was starting to fill the entire room.

Brantley's phone rang and he reached for it. "Hey, Mack," he said happily.

"Have they said anything about when you'll be ready to go?"

"Not yet. They took some blood earlier this morning, and I'm hoping that will be it." He couldn't help smiling at the sound of Mack's rich voice. "I'll call you as soon as they tell me."

"Okay. I'll be there once I get cleaned up, and we can wait together." Mack hung up, and Brantley set his phone back on the tray.

"Sorry," he said. "And I mean it. I know this has to be very hard for you, and I want you to know that you aren't responsible for what he did." Brantley smiled, hoping some reassurance would ease some of the pain and worry on her face.

"I know that," she said softly as she came closer, standing right next to his bed. "There's only one problem," she whispered and placed her hand in the center of Brantley's chest. "My husband, the cheating bastard, didn't have the guts to tell that bitch Renae to mind her own damn business and stay away from what was mine."

In an instant he realized that Julie was behind everything: she'd framed her husband and they'd been completely fooled. Her hand went to Brantley's throat, gripping, but not squeezing, at least not yet, but the threat was enough to keep Brantley from moving.

"Why go after me?" Brantley was confused.

"You're a smart boy—you know why. I needed money, and with you gone, I could mine the creek at will. I've been pulling gold out of it for months now, but I need to go deeper. I kept it all, almost enough to bring the mortgage on my place current, and maybe with a little more work, I can have enough money for a down payment on your place. Then I can mine whenever I want, and no one will look at me twice."

"Why didn't you take what you had and use it to pay for what you needed? No one would have known, and you wouldn't have had to go through all this." The pieces all began to fit into place. Denny hadn't lied about being at Reserves an extra week—that had all been Julie, knowing it would come out. Brantley was willing to bet that Julie was a crack shot with a hunting rifle, and the rest was all her. All she'd needed was a scapegoat, and she got that in her husband, who was cheating on her.

"I couldn't just show up with raw gold and expect there not to be a million questions. I needed to own the location it came from. Gold itself might not be traceable, but raw gold with all the other minerals sure as hell is." Her voice was soft but menacing.

"So you set Denny up to take the fall?" Brantley asked, flicking his gaze in the direction of the door. The curtain had been pulled to block the view, and judging by the quiet, he suspected she'd closed the door when she came in.

"Sure. Why the hell not? He cheated on me, and the sheriff never thought about me. I wore Denny's boots, used his gun, and made sure everything led back to him. I gave him an alibi that I knew would fall apart if anyone looked into it, and from there everything fell into place."

"But where was he?" Brantley placed his hand on hers as she began to squeeze. Julie was a hell of a lot stronger than she looked. He was having some trouble breathing from the pressure. He knew his only chance was to try to buy some time. Mack had said he was going to come up to see him, so if Brantley could keep her talking long enough, he might have a chance. He tried feeling for the call button, but it was gone.

"Denny loves to go camping so he can live off the land. So I suggested he go after the Reserves and then just weaved my story. God, you men are so damn gullible when it comes to women. You never looked twice at me, and my plan was good. Scare you off, frame him for Renae's death." She leaned closer, applied more pressure to his throat, and then eased up. "Hell, when you came home right after I'd taken care of Renae, I called the sheriff, thinking I could throw up some more smoke."

"But why take a shot at me?"

"To scare you off—are you deaf? I thought you had to be close to crapping your pants by then, and when you didn't leave, I knew I had to get rid of you altogether." She smiled and leaned still closer. "You should have seen Mack's face at the fire. I burned you out and talked to him just a few minutes later. He didn't look twice at me, the dumbass. He was so intent on Denny that he never gave me a thought.

Then my asshole husband called to say he was coming home early, and I knew just where to take him out."

"You caused his accident?" Brantley asked, his fear rising to epic proportions. He had to figure a way out of here or he wasn't going to last much longer.

She reached into her pocket, pulled out a sizable syringe, and held it in her hand, showing it off to him.

Brantley stilled. She was going to kill him right here in the hospital, probably using the same stuff she'd used on him before.

"Of course I did. I know this area like the back of my hand. All I had to do was shoot out a tire at the right moment, and he would go over the ravine. It's steep enough that he'd roll at least twice. The fire was a lucky break."

"But you didn't count on Mack getting there so fast," Brantley said.

"Not that it matters. You'll die from something your body makes on its own, and they'll think it was what you were given before. Denny will die of something similar, only they'll think it was his injuries, and I'll play the grieving wife and everything will fall into place, eventually. I may need to do something in order to cash in the gold, but…." She leaned closer, and her eyes were as dark as the depths of hell. "I've gone too far to turn back now."

This had gone way past talking. Brantley figured he was running out of time fast from the way she held the syringe to his neck. She could squeeze and plunge it at the same time, and there wasn't a damn thing he could do about it. "You won't get away with this, and then what about Nathan?" He knew he had to think fast. "He'll be alone."

"My Nathan will be just fine. That's why I'm doing all this. I've thought of everything. Denny will be gone, but Nathan doesn't need a cheating bastard for a father. They half expect him to die anyway, and you'll be written off as a side effect of what *he* gave you earlier. I'll get to Mack as soon as you're out of the picture. I already got the meds. Everything else will work out just fine. I'll be able to save the ranch and can then pass it on to Nathan. He'll have his inheritance, and if things work out, your ranch will be part of it. We'll have the gold and the water, and the ranch will be stable for him. Nothing else is going to matter now. So you can stop your chitchat games and make peace with whatever God you believe in." She thrust the syringe into his arm and depressed the plunger.

Brantley waited for something to happen. He didn't feel anything.

"Now for something to put you to sleep so I can get away...." She reached for another syringe.

Brantley had had enough. If he was going to die, he sure as hell wasn't going to take it lying down.

He grabbed her wrist as hard as he could, pulling it away from his throat. Julie was a strong woman, no doubt about that, and he used all his weight to try to push her back. "I need some help," Brantley yelled. But no one came. He was starting to feel light-headed, and his stomach was extremely unhappy.

She pushed him back and placed her hand over his mouth. He felt her fishing around for something in her pockets, and she came up with another syringe. Brantley banged her hand, and the syringe went flying across the room, landing on the floor.

His hands and legs felt light, and his head began to float. Thinking was becoming more and more difficult. He heard the door open.

"Help," he called and hoped like hell someone heard him. The next thing he knew, the grip on his neck eased, and Julie let loose a steady stream of profanity.

"I was trying to help him," she said.

"No," Brantley croaked, falling deeper and deeper into a black pit. He saw Mack holding her. "She gave me a shot of something," he tried to say. His entire body felt strange, and he knew his ability to think was going fast. Food. All he wanted was food, and there was nothing nearby. His instinct was to reach for the tray, but there was nothing. "Help me, Mack," he said, trying like hell to hold on to consciousness, but it faded away.

CHAPTER 9

MACK HAD come to visit Brantley, and when he stepped into the room and around the curtain, he was horrified to see Julie with her hand at Brantley's throat. He reacted immediately, grabbing her to get her away. Julie fought like the devil, and when Brantley said that she'd injected him with something, he got her arms around her back and pulled upward. He was damn close to breaking her arms, but she still fought like someone possessed.

"Get down on the floor right the hell now," Mack yelled. The room filled with people who had heard his raised voice, and he figured he was seconds from being scolded. "She injected him with something. Find out what it is and help him now!" Mack pulled Julie to the hallway and slammed her against the hallway wall. "Tell me what you gave him."

She shook her head.

"Tell me or so help me I will shoot you right here and say you were grabbing for my gun," he growled, and her eyes filled with fear.

She turned away, and Mack knew he was going to get nothing out of her.

He went through her pockets and found two syringes, one empty and another full. He got the attention of one of the passing nurses and handed her the empty syringe.

"Is this what was used on him?" the nurse asked.

"I think so," Mack said, and she took it and hurried away.

Doctors and nurses passed as Mack held Julie still. He managed to call in and request backup, and was told Ronnie was on his way.

"Like a bat out of hell," Mack responded, and Gloria acknowledged the message. He wanted to be in there to find out if Brantley was going to be all right, but he had to keep Julie under control. More people rushed into Brantley's room, one carrying an IV

166

bag. He had rarely seen people race that fast in a hospital. "What did you give him? If you help me, I might be able to help you."

"Bullshit," Julie said and went quiet.

Mack got her facedown on the floor and checked all her pockets, including the ones in her jacket. "Doctor...," he yelled, and a man came out of Brantley's room. He handed him a small vial, and the doctor hurried back inside. Mack got Julie handcuffed and subdued. He heard Ronnie respond to the radio call, and he appeared a few minutes later, taking charge of Julie. "Get her to the station and put her in a cell. I'll be there as soon as I can." He asked Ronnie for evidence bags and put what he'd found into one.

Zeb showed up as well, and both of them led Julie out of the hospital while Mack took custody of the evidence.

Once Julie was gone, Mack poked his head into Brantley's room. He lay still on the bed and was as pale as the sheets. "What happened?"

"We think she injected him with a massive dose of insulin. We have a glucose IV running, and we've given him some injections. He was responsive a few minutes ago." The doctor checked Brantley again. "Give him one more," he said to the nurse, and she put something into the IV. Then she pricked one of his fingers.

"Fifty," she said when the device she was holding beeped.

"It's coming up," he said. "Get some candy for him. I want him to eat when he wakes up. Also, some orange juice, and add some sugar. He's going to need sugar for a while."

The nurse hurried away, and Mack approached the bed.

"Brantley, can you hear me?" Mack asked, taking his hand. Brantley didn't answer, and Mack turned to the doctor.

"We need to give his body a few minutes. We've pumped a lot of sugar into him to counteract the insulin. It's been coming up, and there's still a steady stream of glucose entering his body."

"Mack?" Brantley whispered. "Is that you?"

"Yes, I'm here." Mack turned as a nurse hurried into the room. "You need to drink this." He took the cup and held the straw to Brantley's lips. "Just drink. It's going to help you."

Brantley sucked in some of the liquid.

167

"You need to keep drinking," the doctor encouraged. "It's going to help you feel better."

Mack continued holding the straw to his lips until Brantley had finished the glass.

"Someone hit me with a baseball bat," Brantley said. "Then they punched me and held me down."

Mack turned to the doctor in confusion.

"It's normal for him to be confused at a time like this. Give it a few minutes." The doctor came closer. "You were injected with a high dose of insulin, and your blood sugar bottomed out. We're going to watch you and keep sugar going into your system for a while, but you should be feeling better really soon." He turned to Mack. "It's a good thing you got here when you did. But I think he's going to be okay now. We'll watch him." The nurses had left, and now the doctor stepped out of the room as well.

"Thanks." Mack turned back to Brantley. "I've made a shit job of it, haven't I?"

Brantley blinked a few times as though he was trying to make sense of what Mack had said. "Why do you say that?" he said much more coherently.

"Because… I was supposed to protect you. All this happened on my watch, and I completely overlooked the one person right out in the open. I suspected every one of your neighbors, but she flew under my radar the entire time."

"I liked her," Brantley said. "If they gave out Academy Awards for criminals, I think she would be up for the lifetime achievement award. She had me completely fooled."

"Me too. But we have her now."

"And she told me everything," Brantley said. "She shot Renae and took the shot at me. She also said she made Denny run off the road. I bet if you search her ranch real good, you'll find the gun and the boots we've been looking for. She said she used both of them."

Wow. Mack wasn't sure what to say. "I thought they were happy."

"She said Denny was having an affair with Renae, and that's why she killed her. She just wanted me out of the way for the ranch, water, and gold." Brantley turned away, and Mack wondered what was going through his mind. It wouldn't surprise him if Brantley decided that New York City was safer than here.

"What are you going to do?" Mack asked.

Brantley sighed and turned back to him. "I don't know. On the one hand, I can rebuild my house and try to make a life in a town where half the people will still think I'm a murderer and some sort of freak for being gay, or I can go back to New York, where my professional reputation is in tatters." He closed his eyes.

"There is one thing, and I hope it's important, that you didn't take into consideration," Mack said.

"I took everything into consideration." Brantley opened his startling blue eyes and looked deeply into Mack's. "I think you go a long way toward tipping the scales in favor of this town."

"So you're going to stay?"

"Yes. I'm going to find an architect and have a house designed that will be exactly what I want, with plenty of wood and windows to let in the light, as well as a room to display my art collection."

Mack leaned over the bed. "Can you afford all that? I know you have money, but…."

"I'm easily the richest person in town, and maybe in the top five in the state. I was very good at making money for my clients, and they paid me a great deal for the privilege. Does that make a difference to you?"

Mack had known Brantley had money, but that much money was hard for him to visualize. "Only that I don't want you to think I'm interested in you for what you have."

Brantley squeezed his hand and smiled. "I don't. So this thing is really over?"

"Yes. I need to go to the station and take care of Julie. It's going to be a paperwork nightmare, but your testimony will help a great deal."

Brantley nodded slowly. "Be sure to stop in and see Denny. He's going to need friends now, and so is Nathan."

The impact on that little boy hit Mack almost as hard as the realization of how close he'd come to losing Brantley… again. That was becoming a habit that Mack desperately wanted to break. "I have to go," he said softly.

"I know. Hopefully once they have figured out how to counteract what Julie did, I can go home. I'm tired of lying here."

Mack kissed Brantley once again and then turned toward the door. "Call me as soon as you know anything, and I'll get back over here." He left the room and used his position to get Denny's room number. Mack went right there, pausing outside the room before entering. His old friend lay on the bed, pale and looking as though he hadn't shaved in a few days. Mack sat next to the bed, watching his chest slowly rise and fall.

"I saved you yesterday. To do my job, I had to put our friendship aside. But now I know there's nothing to worry about." Mack was more relieved than he ever wanted to admit. Arresting his old friend had been the last thing he'd wanted to do, and he was grateful he now didn't have to.

Denny groaned. "What are you talking about?" His words were barely audible.

Mack jumped up and then called the nurse. "He's waking up," he told the young man when he came into the room.

"Thanks goodness. I'll call the doctor."

"Where's Julie? Why isn't she here?" Denny asked.

Of course Denny had no idea what had been happening or what his wife had been up to, and it would fall on Mack's shoulders to break his friend's world into small pieces.

"She can't be here right now, so I was stopping by to check on you," Mack said, watching as Denny's eyes fluttered open.

"Where am I?"

"In the hospital," Mack explained. "Your truck went off the road and flipped a couple times. I pulled you out, and they brought you here." He figured there was plenty of time to tell him everything, but not at this very moment.

"Was Nathan with me?"

"No. You were alone." Mack reminded himself that he needed to find out where Nathan was and make sure there was someone who could take care of him until Denny was able to. "Just relax and rest. Everything is going to be all right now."

Denny nodded and closed his eyes.

The nurses and doctors came, and Mack explained about their conversation, getting out of the way so they could do their jobs. When he went to leave, the doctor took him aside. "Should we tell him about his wife?" the doctor asked.

"No. I have some things to do in regard to her. I'll be back in a few hours, and I'll sit down and explain everything to him then. Just let him rest and recuperate."

"He's going to sleep for hours yet, so... I'll make sure that instructions are left."

"Thank you," Mack said firmly and then left the hospital.

"THANKS FOR coming to get me," Brantley said when Mack picked him up at the hospital early that evening. "How did it all go?"

"Paperwork by the ton," Mack said. "Julie is safely behind bars in my jail, and that's where she's going to stay. She tried to put the ranch up as collateral for her bail, but once they found out that her husband was a victim in all this as well, that died on the vine."

"What about Nathan?"

"He's home with his buddy Lew and the dogs. This afternoon after I popped my head in to see you, I explained everything that had happened to Denny. Things between him and Julie weren't good at all. It turns out that Julie was abusive, and Denny was too much of a gentleman to fight back. He was preparing to leave her but hadn't yet because of Nathan."

"My God."

"Exactly. Julie had suggested he go camping to clear his head and then used his time away against him." Mack pulled to a stop and turned to Brantley, relieved to have him home and in one piece. The doctor had said he had to take it easy and made him promise to eat regularly in case there were any aftereffects from the insulin injection. "The kicker is that he says he never had an affair with Renae. They were friends of a sort, and he was seeing her for advice on how to save the ranch."

"Jesus, that is so fucked up. Renae is dead because Julie got it all wrong."

"Yup. I'm having her evaluated by a doctor to head off some insanity defense." Mack pulled back onto the road and continued to his house.

"How did she know about the insulin and get access to the drugs?"

"Her mother is diabetic, and Julie took some of her supplies. The other stuff she got from taking care of the horses and cattle. By the way, I moved your things into my room. Denny is going to be in the hospital a few more days, but now that he's awake, he's going to be okay. Erickson is taking care of things at the ranch. I hope it's okay, but I pulled in one of the many favors he owes you to get him to do it."

"Of course," Brantley said just as Mack had expected him to. "We should try to help our neighbors when we can."

Mack pulled into the drive and stopped. He and Brantley got out and walked slowly up to the door. "Hey, Dad," Mack said when he entered, and Lew shushed him quickly.

Nathan was asleep on the sofa, curled on his side.

"I made some soup," Lew whispered. "So come through to the kitchen when you're ready."

Mack followed Brantley down the hall to his room, and they went inside. Mack closed the door and tugged Brantley to him. "You've given me more scares in the past few days." He kissed him hard, needing to touch and taste and know that Brantley was truly okay.

"I'm fine, Mack," Brantley said when they pulled apart a minute later. "But you can do that anytime." Brantley rested his head on Mack's shoulder, and they stood together, quietly. "I have to ask what you plan to do if you don't win the next election."

"Seems like a weird time for that conversation," Mack said.

172

"I know. But having me in your life could cost you a lot. And don't tell me it's no big deal. I know you love what you do, and I don't want to be the cause of you losing something that important."

"Hey. You are important. Being sheriff is a job. If I lose reelection, then I'll probably turn rancher and work alongside a certain newcomer from back East." Mack winked. "If you're willing, we'll just take things one step at a time and do what needs to be done. Yes, there will be people who won't vote for me, but I'd like to think most people aren't going to care."

"Are you sure?" Brantley asked, and Mack closed the last small gap between them until they were chest to chest, Brantley's erection pressing to Mack's own. "I guess you are."

"Everything will work out one way or another." Mack was thrilled when Brantley quivered in his arms.

"WHAT ABOUT Nathan and his dad?" Brantley asked from on top of the covers as Mack sat on the edge of the bed. He had been like the grand inquisitor for the last hour.

"Tomorrow we're going to take Nathan up to see his dad, and hopefully Denny will be able to come home in a few days. Lew is going to come along. Nathan has really bonded with him and is calling him Grandpa Lew, so I think that's best. We can explain about his mother then." It damn near broke Mack's heart every time Nathan asked where his mother was. "This whole thing is a real mess."

"No. It's a challenge. The real mess has been unraveled and brought to light. People can deal with it now, and hopefully they'll rally around Denny and Nathan rather than turn away from them." Mack pulled the covers up around them and lay next to Brantley, holding him close. God, he needed this. He stroked down his back, rememorizing the contours, especially that slight dip just before the curve of Brantley's ass.

"Your dad is going to be waiting for us," Brantley said even as he hugged Mack tighter with a soft sigh. "They said I need to eat, but I'm not hungry for food."

"How about you eat some soup, and then we'll concentrate on other activities." Mack was determined that the incident from earlier in the day would be out of Brantley's system. He pulled away, caressing up Brantley's back and then letting his hands drift away. "Come on. Let's eat." He took Brantley's hand and led him out of the room.

As Mack expected, Lew had a million questions, and Mack answered what he could. There were some he wasn't prepared to talk about, especially with regard to evidence. He also didn't want to talk about Nathan's mother directly, in case the boy woke up, so they talked in a code of sorts.

"Grandpa Lew?" Nathan came into the kitchen rubbing his eyes, and Mack's dad rolled back. Nathan climbed on his lap. "Where's Mama and Daddy?"

"Your daddy was hurt, but he's doing better, and we're going to take you to see him tomorrow," Mack told him.

"Are you hungry?" Lew asked, and Nathan nodded.

Brantley stood and got him a bowl and some crackers, then brought them to the table.

Nathan ate without getting down, and he kept looking at all of them as though he knew something was very wrong and was waiting for them to tell him. "Where's my mama?" Nathan turned and asked Lew, who glanced at the others, looking for an answer.

Mack sighed. "Your mama tried to hurt people really bad."

"Is she in jail?" Nathan asked.

Mack was shocked into silence for a second, wondering if Nathan had overheard something, but then maybe that was a logical conclusion for a youngster. People who hurt people went to jail. "Yes, she is. Your daddy will tell you all about it, I promise." He'd hoped to be able to avoid the topic altogether, but he wasn't going to lie to him. "Why don't you eat your soup, and then you can play or watch television before bed."

Nathan took a few bites and then leaned back against his Grandpa Lew's chest.

Lew hugged him and slowly rolled away from the table. "It's all right. You'll see your daddy tomorrow." Lew left the room with Nathan, and Mack turned to Brantley.

"How are we going to make things okay for him?" Mack asked. "What happened is going to stay with him forever."

"I know." Brantley finished his soup and took his dishes to the sink. Then he left the room without saying anything else.

Mack finished his own dinner and did all the dishes. He needed some time to think. Catching the bad guy was his job, and he'd done that, but in the process, he'd left a four-year-old without a mother. That wasn't his fault, but it didn't mean it wasn't the complete shits.

He heard the unmistakable music of cartoons and hoped Nathan was content. When Mack was finished, he joined them in the living room.

"Brantley went to bed."

It was too early for him to go to sleep, so he sat with his father and Nathan, watching some show about Princess Sophia until Nathan fell asleep. Mack put Nathan to bed, his heart breaking for the little boy.

Lew was waiting for him when he left the bedroom. "Your feelings for him do you credit," Lew said. "It's easy to be heartless." He looked toward the master bedroom. "If you and Brantley decide to have children someday, you'll be a very good father."

"Dad, we haven't known each other that long. Isn't it a little soon to talk like that?"

"After your mother left, I had to be both parents to you. I think that experience gave me a very good insight into you. Maybe better than your own. But the thing is, you and I, we expect people to leave. It's what your mother did, and that stayed with us."

Mack nodded. That had been in the back of his mind ever since he'd met Brantley. Even now, he expected him to change his mind and decide to go back to New York. "What do I do?"

"You live your life. Brantley has had plenty of chances to leave, and he hasn't. Lord knows that boy has reason to. But he's asleep in your room, and I dare say he's waiting for you to come to bed. To be with him. That says a lot. Brantley is strong and knows his mind. So all you have to do is accept it."

"It's that simple?"

"Yup. I never stopped loving your mother and didn't move on. Some people would say that was a mistake, but I don't regret it. You, on the other hand, have a chance with Brantley. Don't hesitate to open your heart to him just because you're afraid he'll do to you what your mother did to me."

"It's...."

"Just let yourself be happy for today… a week… a year… the rest of your life. Take what comes and you could hit the jackpot." Lew turned in his chair, heading toward his bedroom, and Mack quietly opened the door to his bedroom.

The air smelled of Brantley as he went inside and closed the door. Mack stripped off his clothes and climbed into the bed as gently as he could so he didn't disturb…. He wasn't sure how to finish that thought.

"Mack…," Brantley said softly.

"Yes," Mack said as he rolled onto his side. "Are you feeling okay?"

Brantley slid right next to him, pressing his heated body to Mack's. "I love you." Brantley paused, and Mack swallowed hard. "I know we've said things to each other, but I wanted you to know. Falling in love wasn't what I expected after a week like this, but I do love you, and I want you in my life."

"I love you too." Mack brought his lips to Brantley's, kissing him harder than he intended, but the energy between them drew him in. "I know it's fast…."

"Slow… fast… doesn't matter. What does is that we found each other." Brantley kissed him once again, pressing Mack onto his back as he climbed on top of him. "I've had many hours to rest and think about what I want."

"Are you sure?" Mack asked.

"Yes. Are you?" Brantley asked in return.

Mack let his kiss answer for him, and soon they were showing each other just how much they cared and needed each other. Minutes and hours fused together in the dark room that was their sanctuary from what had happened and what was still to be done. They explored with tongues and hands and learned what was still new, and when Mack entered Brantley's body, slowly filling him, he found himself equally filled with the care and love that had blossomed between them and burst outward to fill the entire room. He was going to hold on to this for the rest of his life. Of that he had no doubt.

Epilogue

A Year Later

"It took so much longer than I expected," Brantley said as he stood out in front of his property, looking at his newly completed home, which they'd just moved into. It was exactly what he'd hoped for and more. He'd built it low to the ground, using local stone and roofing that took its colors from the surrounding area, so the house looked like an extension of the land. A large porch ran the entire length of the front and around the side of the house, furnished for hours of conversation and evening lounging.

"Was it worth it?" Mack asked, slipping an arm around his waist.

"Yes. We have the main house, and your dad has his own rooms." Brantley had insisted on building a suite for Lew with extra-large rooms so he could easily maneuver his chair around the bed and other furniture.

"Dad thinks he's died and gone to heaven. And the family who bought my house was thrilled to pieces, so everything worked out."

Brantley wished other things had worked out as well. Word had gotten out that gold had been found in the creek. His first instinct was to let people look, but when one of the yokels decided he was going to bring in digging equipment, Brantley had been forced to close off the path across his property from the street. It sucked that one person's stupidity and greed had ended a fun thing for everyone.

A beep sounded, and Brantley guided Mack away from the drive as a familiar dark blue truck with the Soaring Eagle Ranch logo emblazoned on the side pulled in. Brantley hadn't wanted to use his name for the ranch, and when a pair of eagles had decided to nest in the trees near the spring, he'd taken it as a sign. "Uncle Brantley,"

178

Nathan cried as he climbed out of the truck and raced over to where they were standing.

Brantley scooped him up, swinging him around in circles to the sound of giggles and laughter that made his heart soar. "Did you have fun camping with your daddy?"

"Yes. We saw a fox and some birds, and the eagles made loud noises. Daddy said they were trying to scare off anything that got close to their babies. We cooked out and made hot dogs, and I roasted them over the fire." Nathan chattered on about everything as fast as he could, barely stopping to take a breath.

"It sounds like you had a good time." Brantley got a hug, and then Nathan squirmed over to Mack for another one.

"We did," Denny said, walking over to where they stood. There were deep lines around his eyes and mouth that now seemed like permanent fixtures. "The D-I-V-O-R-C-E is final and done," he said. "That part of our lives is over."

Even from prison, Julie had tried to fight it, but she'd gotten no traction and only delayed the inevitable. Denny had been awarded all the assets, and in the end, Julie got nothing but a life sentence without the possibility of parole in a prison on the far side of the state. Brantley knew that Mack had called in a favor to get her placed as far away as possible. Denny thought it best that Nathan be given the chance to heal as much as possible. Brantley gave Denny credit—he'd answered all of Nathan's questions honestly, and in the end, Nathan had clung to his father and now only rarely asked about his mother, who had lost custody of her son as part of the divorce settlement.

"Time to move on, then," Brantley said, "and I have just the thing."

"You do?"

"Yeah. I want to expand the herd in a huge way. We've started slowly the last year, but it's time we make the ranch a real going concern. So hire who you need, and let's get to it."

"You're serious," Denny said.

"You better believe it. You're more than capable of running a large cattle operation, so let's build one."

Denny's financial issues had been too much to overcome, so Brantley had bought his ranch rather than have it return to the bank, and he'd made Denny the manager of all the land. He and Nathan had stayed in their home, and Brantley had instantly acquired expert cattle knowledge. Brantley already had the business acumen needed. It was a win for all of them.

"I heard Gunther is looking to retire and sell up. He has great stock," Denny said.

"See if he's interested in selling, and I'll negotiate a price," Brantley said. "You're going to need more hands other than William, so start hiring as we need them."

Mack had thought he was a little crazy at the time, but Brantley had hired on William Turner, the veteran who'd shown up in town, to help him get his life together, and it turned out he was an amazing worker.

"We might need a bunkhouse," Denny said, since William still lived in town in housing the church had helped him get.

"Then we'll build one, and maybe a treehouse for this guy while we're at it." Brantley tickled Nathan's belly, and he giggled before throwing his arms in the air in a show of joy and excitement. "Supper will be in an hour, and I'm cooking. So go home to get things put away and then come on back. We've got plenty to talk about."

Mack nudged his arm and nodded. "I forgot. I was going to ask about a horse operation. Do you think we should do something along that line?"

Denny appeared thoughtful, and his expression told Brantley all he needed to know. "How about we do one thing well and get it up and running before branching out."

"Excellent," Brantley agreed, and Denny took Nathan and carried him back toward the truck. He and Mack waved before they walked to the house and went inside.

"How in the hell do you manage to do that?"

"What?" Brantley asked.

"Their lives had been ripped to pieces, and you manage to come in and put it all back together without them even realizing that's what you're doing. Nathan is happy, and Denny is getting on with his life. It hasn't been that long, and they're already settled. Julie's imprint on them is fading quickly."

"She did that herself. I just recognized talent and scooped it up when I had the chance." Brantley pulled open the heavy wooded front door and stepped into what to his mind was perfection: warm wood, large windows, plenty of light, thick rugs, and carefully designed rustic details that hid the most modern of everything. Brantley loved his conveniences.

Other things had changed for him, including the addition of the two large mutts that danced around their legs, vying for attention. He and Mack took turns greeting Kit and Carson, as well as the other three dogs, before they all wandered off to see if there was anything new in their bowls. Brantley had been surprised at how easily he'd adjusted to life in the West. His tastes in many things had altered.

"Have you decided what you're going to do with the gallery space you had built?" Mack asked as they settled down onto one of the amazingly comfortable living room sofas. As part of the design of the house, he'd built a gallery so he could display his art collection. But it hadn't seemed to fit with the surroundings, so he'd sold all of them at auction and was starting something new.

"Not yet. But I saw a piece I wanted." Brantley pulled out his tablet and showed Mack a picture from the auction listing. "It's four feet high, and I thought I'd build a pedestal to display it in the center of the room. It's called *The Sheriff*, and when I saw it, it reminded me of you." Brantley showed Mack the image of the figure in bronze. "To me you will always be the sheriff, the lawman who stole my heart."

Mack's reelection had gone remarkably well in November. "What if I decide I don't want to run next time?"

Kit jumped on the sofa and settled next to Brantley, nuzzling for attention, while Carson stretched out on the floor at their feet.

"Then you can do whatever you want to do," Brantley said. "Lew said you used to love horses. So maybe you can take on the horse breeding when we get around to it. Who knows? I have a million ideas, and right now most of them center around us doing unspeakable things to one another."

Mack leaned closer, his weight pressing Brantley back. Kit jumped down with a huff, and Brantley fished around to set the tablet on the floor. Mack slotted his mouth over Brantley's, tugging at his lips while he pushed him down onto the cushions. "Maybe we should take this to the bedroom," Mack said, turning aside.

Brantley followed his gaze to the two dogs sitting a few feet away, staring at them. "Not a bad idea."

"And as for unspeakable things," Mack segued. "You know with me nothing is unspeakable. I'll tell you exactly what I want to do to you and how loudly I want to hear you scream."

As they'd gotten closer, Mack had gotten more and more vocal in the bedroom. It was a real turn-on, and Brantley had no desire to change that behavior in any way.

"How about you put your money where your mouth is," Brantley said and took off, with Mack right behind him. By the time he reached the bedroom, they were both laughing like idiots, even as Mack pulled Brantley's shirt over his head. Giggles turned to moans and shivers when Mack latched onto one of his nipples, sending heat coursing through him.

Brantley ran his fingers through Mack's hair, pulling it free so it could flow almost to his shoulders. He loved the way Mack's soft locks slipped between his fingers. "Damn, I love you," Brantley hissed as Mack scraped his teeth over his hard bud and then went for the other one. Mack tightened his grip around his waist and drove him wild with his tongue. Brantley's legs shook like one of the dogs when he petted them, the energy Mack was generating too much for him to contain.

"I love you too," Mack told him, pushing Brantley back down onto the bed. "I intend to love you and love on you for the rest of my life. So hang on and prepare for one hell of a ride." Mack gazed deeply into his eyes, Brantley returning the fire he saw in them— something he'd never get tired of.

"It's always a hell of a ride with you."

"Me? I was referring to you. You're one who's always full of surprises." Mack kissed away Brantley's protest, and the sizzle between them built to epic heights. Mack knew just where to touch and how to tease until Brantley's brain short-circuited. "You're the one who put this entire ranch together in a year and somehow made everyone happy."

"Not everyone, because you make me happy," Brantley said, thrusting his hips forward to catch any friction he could.

"Then how about this, sweetheart? I'll go about making you happy forever, and you do the same for me."

Brantley grunted his response when Mack tugged at his pants. That was the deal of the century, and he could more than live with it.

DIRK is very much an outside kind of man. He loves travel and seeing new things. Dirk worked in corporate America for way too long and now spends his days writing, gardening, and taking care of the home he shares with his partner of more than two decades. He has a master's degree and all the other accessories that go with a corporate job. But he is most proud of the stories he tells and the life he's built. Dirk lives in Pennsylvania in a century-old home and is blessed with an amazing circle of friends.

Facebook: www.facebook.com/dirkgreyson
E-mail: dirkgreyson@comcast.net

AN
ASSASSIN'S
HOLIDAY

DIRK
GREYSON

Brick Colton has been hired to kill Santa Claus—or at least the kindhearted accountant playing Santa for the kids in an orphanage. Brick grew up in an orphanage himself, but that isn't the only thing bothering him about the contract on Robin Marvington's life. The details don't add up, and it's looking more and more like someone has set Robin up. As Brick investigates, Robin brings some much-needed cheer into his life, the light in Robin's soul reaching something in Brick's dark one. But all of that will end if they can't find the person who wants Robin dead.

www.dreamspinnerpress.com

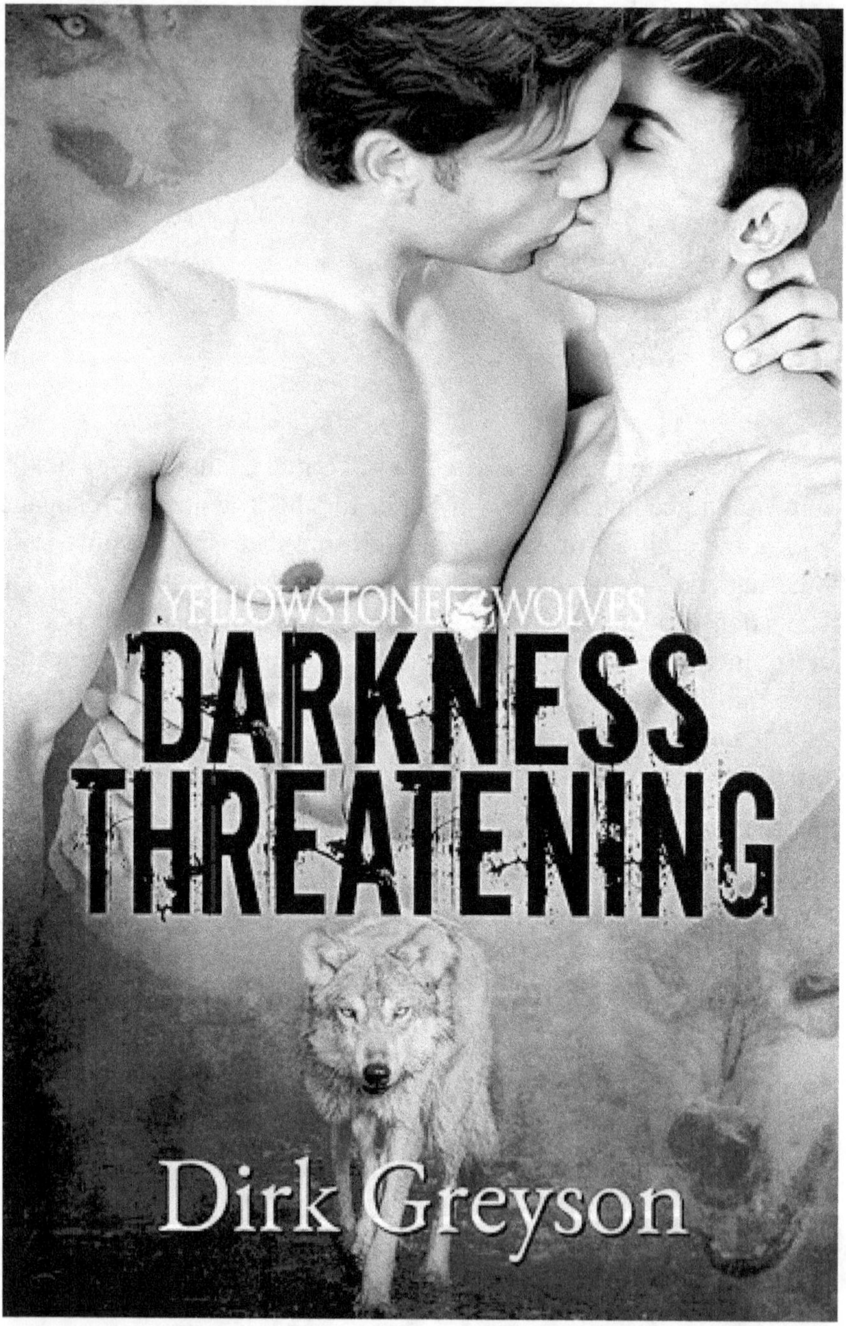
YELLOWSTONE WOLVES
DARKNESS
THREATENING
Dirk Greyson

Sequel to *Challenge the Darkness*
Yellowstone Wolves: Book 2

Fredrik is back from college and trying to stay out of his power-hungry brother's way, until his brother takes a prisoner for his pleasure. Unable to tolerate his family's cruelty, Fredrik overcomes his fear to help her escape back to her pack. There, he meets Christopher, and their instant attraction tells him Christopher is the one. However, since the threat of his brother remains, Fredrik is reluctant to pursue a relationship.

Christopher is still figuring out his place in the pack and has been living on his own to avoid making waves with his brother, Mikael. Now he's met his soulmate, and he'll do anything to take care of his love, including rejoining the pack.

With coaxing, Fredrik accepts his feelings, and Christopher's pack gives him the home he's never had. But Fredrick soon realizes he should keep running. His brother is on his tail and will stop at nothing to obtain the power he craves, especially when he realizes the source of the power could be Fredrik himself.

www.dreamspinnerpress.com

Sequel to *Sun and Shadow*
Day and Knight: Book 3

For Scorpion agents Day and Knight, their relationship is slow to develop, and trust is hard to build. Then Day's brother, Stephen, goes missing, and Day finds out more about him than he ever dreamed. Day's first reaction to Stephen's disappearance is to try to get to him as fast as possible.

Knight initially holds him back so they can attempt to find out what they're walking into. But when Knight sees Day's desperation, he steps in to help and tries to calm the man he's growing to care about, even though the trail is cold and clues are scarce.

When Day witnesses his brother being shot live on television, he loses the last of his control. Despite the lack of answers, Day is more determined than ever to find out what happened. Stephen was all the family he had left.

Bone-deep fear and adversity threaten to tear Day and Knight apart, but facing unimaginable hardship together might finally cement the bond between them.

www.dreamspinnerpress.com